T0380250

For Pete's Sake

A Novel

ROD LEE

ROD LEE
For Pete's Sake

AuthorHouse™
1663 Liberty Drive
Bloomington, IN 47403
www.authorhouse.com
Phone: 1 (800) 839-8640

Because of the dynamic nature of the Internet, any web addresses or links contained in this book may have changed since publication and may no longer be valid. The views expressed in this work are solely those of the author and do not necessarily reflect the views of the publisher, and the publisher hereby disclaims any responsibility for them.

Any people depicted in stock imagery provided by Getty Images are models, and such images are being used for illustrative purposes only.
Certain stock imagery © Getty Images.

This book is printed on acid-free paper.

FIRST EDITION

ISBN: 978-1-7283-6097-3 (sc)
ISBN: 978-1-7283-6096-6 (e)

Library of Congress Control Number: 2020908179

Print information available on the last page.

Published by AuthorHouse 05/08/2020

authorHOUSE®

To Doris Marie (Joiner) Lee, Amanda Marie (Lee) Peloquin, Daniel James Lee and Caroline Noel Lee, with a husband and father's enduring love

'All growth is a leap in the dark, a spontaneous unpremeditated act without the benefit of experience'

—Henry Miller

'The search after the great is the dream of youth, and the most serious occupation of manhood.'

—Ralph Waldo Emerson

CONTENTS

INTRODUCTION

Skeptics and detractors would probably say "what on earth were you thinking? If not at the beginning, then certainly now when my part in the life of the family drama is nearing a close. They would point to the carnage that I am principally responsible for and say "you should have left well enough alone. Your wife, your children, deserved better. You put yourself ahead of them and what have you got to show for it?" They would be right, too. Given the chance to reply (which I am now, in the pages that follow), I would tell them I have said the very same things to myself over and over, since moving the family east in 1985.

I am in fact my own worst critic.

I remember what it was like, how good we had it. Marie in her dream house, the one my father built for her with his carpenter-contractor hands, in her childhood hometown. Amanda, at fifteen, shy and sensitive and yet on the verge of flowering into the young woman she was meant to be. Daniel, at eleven, adventurous, free to roam the neighborhood on his bicycle with his cousin Joey, free to pursue the activities that mark a growing boy's youth. Caroline, at ten, already exhibiting the independence and spunk that had made her the most popular girl on the street—able to collect friends as someone would collect commemorative coins or special stamps. All of them cloistered in the bosom of a small community that posed no danger, with grandparents close by to smother them with attention and love; aunts and uncles and cousins to make their birthday parties and Christmases and other holidays extra meaningful.

As for myself, I also would have had no reason to complain. I was news editor of the local daily in Binghamton, a publication with a long reach, across Broome County and beyond. My job was secure—or so it seemed. I had taken up interests that gave me satisfaction: gardening, bowling, golfing, crafting early American furniture, home projects, walking, buying and listening to vinyl records, acquiring books, discovering finds at garage sales around town.

Some would attribute my decision, arrived at hastily but with a conviction that it was the correct one, to a midlife crisis. I did not see it that way. For me, it was mostly a case of feeling stifled—unfulfilled.

I wanted more.

For me, "Boston calling" was the excitement of stepping onto a new frontier. I seized the opportunity. I accepted the repercussions that came with it, for leaving Vestal.

This, then, is "our story," a true (fictionalized) account of the ordeal the five of us—the Lee's (the Nash's)—have gone through in exchanging one locale for another. It is rendered with what I like to think of as unsparing honesty. Aspects of it, including ones being revealed here for the first time, in explaining my motivations, will be unsettling to those personally affected.

I can only hope that in reading For Pete's Sake, the people I care most about will recognize the main characters as having been drawn with a sympathetic brush (excluding, for reasons that will become apparent, myself.

It is, when all is said and done, a love story.

--R.L.

Linwood, Massachusetts

January 2020

CHAPTER ONE
MADDIE NASH, IN FLIGHT

October 1985

She began her journey by taking a single step, as the old adage says a person must; this on an autumn night with a hint of frost in the air.

Not of a thousand miles, but three hundred.

Madeline Anne Nash was fifteen years old when she left the house in the Grafton Hill neighborhood of Worcester, Massachusetts and set foot in the direction she had been instructed to take. The sidewalk on which she made her way was bumpy and uneven and still wet from afternoon rains, and strewn with leaves, which made for a slippery trek. But this was of little concern to her. It was, she surmised, a small price to pay for the opportunity to break free.

She was wearing high-top sneakers (white with black laces), blue jeans (frayed at the ankles) and a green and gold-hooded sweatshirt with the name of her former school—Vestal—superimposed on the outline of a bear standing on its hind legs and roaring; as if about to engage in a pitched battle with an enemy. Man or beast.

The bear was the school's mascot and a symbol of the varsity football team's fearsome "short-punt" formation, from which the quarterback operated as a free-ranging runner or passer behind a line of sturdy blockers.

"Those farm boys," people in the weathered wooden bleachers on the Clayton Avenue side of the stadium chimed, in appreciation of the "three yards and a cloud of dust" attack that Coach Dick Hoover's squads were known for.

"They can hit like nobody's business."

Maddie Nash was not particularly athletic or fond of football, but floodlit Vestal Memorial Stadium was the place to be on Friday nights at seven o'clock. Maddie knew this, just as she knew that to be seen at the shopping center in Johnson City was another validation that one "belonged." It wasn't so much being part of a clique or a class and thus a notch above others of lesser means as it was being identified with a way of life that presented itself as "normal." Follow the Bears, shop at Sears,

Dick's Sporting Goods (which got its start in the area), in the Oakdale Mall or Walmart on the Parkway, dine at the Vestal Steak House or at the Red Lion or Tony's Pizza across the river in Endicott and you would be assured an adulthood like that of your parents. One that was unmarred by problems that would prove to be your undoing.

Anywhere in Worcester, Massachusetts, a whole different story.

II

Maddie had sixty-seven dollars in her pocket and a determination to make it to the bus depot on Madison Street, less than two miles away. The money that she had scraped together for a one-way ticket to Binghamton was all she carried with her, so as not to raise suspicions about what she was up to. She had thought of throwing a few things into a pillow case and slinging it over her shoulder in the mold of a traditional runaway but had then decided against it. Her sole objective was to slip out undetected.

Julia Cruz who was the only friend Maddie had managed to acquire during her brief time in Massachusetts had given her thirty-five dollars towards her fare and mapped out for her on a piece of notebook paper the route she would need to follow to catch the 10:10 Peter Pan bus—the last of the evening.

"I'd show you but I can't be out at that hour. My father would beat the crap out of me," Julia had said.

"It's okay, don't worry about it," Maddie had replied. "Thanks for the help."

Julia Cruz, who was Puerto Rican. "I didn't know a single Hispanic girl or boy, in Vestal," Maddie had told herself more than once. "Goes to show how out of place I am in this godforsaken city."

Still, Julia had been good to her. Maddie wasn't sure why, only that someone like Julia, who knew her way around, how to handle herself, was an important ally.

So here she was, heading up Farrar St., alone in a grimy old industrial city (the second largest in all of New England) that sprawled across "Seven Hills," that teemed with its allotment of crime and corruption, that swallowed innocents like Maddie Nash with hardly a blink of hesitation; or remorse. A city made more austere by the fact that she didn't fit.

Maddie's father could have scoured the ends of the earth and not found a place more different and more frightening from Vestal, than Worcester. It was not just the bigness, the vastness. That alone would have been enough to set her nerves on edge. Without even knowing the full extent of Worcester's breadth, its yawning immensity from the north bordering Holden and West Boylston to the south bordering Auburn and Millbury, from the east nestled against Grafton and Shrewsbury and from the west next door to Leicester and Paxton, she was conscious of being in over her head.

The Vestal she knew had come to be defined by a four-lane highway—"the Parkway"—stretching east toward the state university and the city of Binghamton; just as her father's had been defined by "the Avenue" in Endicott. His youth had been spent in the stores and movie theaters on either side of Washington Avenue, hers in and around the Parkway with its increasingly commercial feel—as such enterprises as Red Lobster, Olive Garden and Barnes & Noble gobbled up real estate.

As a boy Pete Nash had not ventured much farther than a few miles from his house in West Corners, usually on his trusty Schwinn. Similarly, Maddie Nash had found all of the comforts and reinforcements she needed within easy reach.

Growing up, neither of them had felt insecure in or threatened by their surroundings.

Her mind spun, trying to make sense of what evil forces had conspired to deposit her in such as austere setting as Worcester.

She fought the urge to shiver.

III

Maddie was not afraid. She knew she should have been. The real danger though lay in continuing to attend the high school on Harrington Way: the high school her father had said would be a suitable replacement for the one she had frequented back home. *What did he know about the hostile surroundings into which she'd been thrust?* It was like nothing she could have imagined, so stark a contrast from what she was familiar with. Blacks, whites, Italians, Irish, Armenians, Greeks, Latinos and Asians toughened on the streets of a city of 170,000 who were constantly vying for control of the classrooms and the hallways of the building with their bravado, their fists and their knives. She felt like an outcast. *How could dad have thought that a shy and sensitive small-town girl who had been accustomed to a cocoon-like existence, awash in the love of grandparents, aunts and uncles and cousins all of whom lived nearby, would be able to survive in such a cesspool?*

Doesn't he know that I am prone to crying at the slightest bruise to my tender soul?

Maddie was the eldest of Pete and Mary Lou's three children. Donald Jeremiah "DJ" Nash was born four years after her, in January of 1974, Katherine Rose—"Kate"—a year later. There was an instant bond between the three of them. DJ and Kate cared deeply for their big sister, recognizing in her a fragility of composition like that of fine china and a purity of spirit like that of Snow White. Notwithstanding the punch to the stomach that DJ had delivered to her one night when her parents had gone to a movie and he couldn't get his own way, leaving her with a belly ache for weeks to come, and the machete from a family trip to Mexico he had wielded on another occasion, they were bound by a mutual affection. They were also united in the fall of '85 by an apprehension about the move from upstate New York to Central Massachusetts. The specter of being uprooted had filled them with a sense of dread about the future. There was in each of their hearts a certainty that disaster awaited them.

Mary Lou (Jenkins) Nash shared their concern. She was being yanked from her "forever house," the first that she and Pete had owned. It was a still-new center-entrance Colonial sided in her favorite color—red—and situated in close proximity to that of her parents and the Methodist church she'd frequented since childhood. Mary Lou's older sister and reliable confidante Sarah Sweeney lived just around the corner.

In her quest for secrecy Maddie had not told DJ and Kate of her intentions. They understood, however, how angry she was. Seeing the two-story structure from the Farrar St. side of the property when her parents introduced the children to the house that August, she was overcome by a surge of revulsion. The dirty white siding was crumpled in places. Several pieces of it were dislodged. The small porch to the side door was falling apart, as was the one in front, facing Cohasset St., she would discover. The short driveway sloping up to a detached one-bay garage was a mish mash of disintegrated asphalt.

The garage leaned! *I swear it does*, she thought.

"Dad, how could you?" Maddie said, thinking of her paternal grandfather, a framing carpenter all his life.

"Grampa Nash built mom the home she is supposed to be in. He would not believe this!"

"It's the best we could do," Pete said, trying to sound positive. He and Mary Lou had checked out apartments and houses in and around Boston. In Somerville, in Natick, in Brockton. They were all too expensive. The Commonwealth's economy was booming, girded by a workforce that had been swelled by an influx of financial wizards, development hotshots, food-industry impresarios, brainy educators, tech-savvy computer geeks, hotel magnates, biomedical researchers, venture capitalists and advertising and public-relations wizards. The governor, Michael S. Dukakis, was trumpeting the phenomenon as "the Massachusetts Miracle"—and getting the kind of national buzz that would lead to a bid for the presidency.

Finally the realtor Mary Lou was working with suggested homes for sale forty miles west of the newspaper office on Harvard St. in Brookline where Pete was already working.

"Everyone here commutes to the Hub," she had said, encouragingly. "Some from as far away as southern New Hampshire and the Cape."

Mary Lou liked the price tag of $89,000. She liked the kitchen, which although worn was large enough for her purposes as an enthusiast of cooking and baking. The kitchen was equipped with lots of cupboards and shelves. The wallpaper, adorned with apples, was a plus. She liked the handsome scrolled molding in the living room and dining room. She could accept the upstairs bathroom with its cast-iron, claw-footed tub even though it was too small and outdated. She could live with the dirt-floor cellar because she wouldn't be venturing there anyway.

Weighing the pros and cons in the same practical manner her no-nonsense father, Albert "Pa" Jenkins, would have employed, she felt her knees buckle. Burying her pride and the disappointment that felt as if it was suffocating her, she said "we'll take it."

IV

Maddie loved her father. She was "daddy's girl" from the moment she was born in a hospital in Plattsburgh, at the edge of Lake Champlain, in March of 1970. At one and two and three with her walnut-colored hair cut "Annie"-style she knew, instinctively, that Pete would protect her from harm. That he would share with Mary Lou the task of changing her diapers (just as Mary Lou shared with Maddie the crafting of paper hearts—an activity Maddie enjoyed). That he would bounce her on his knee. That he, like Mary Lou, would spare no effort in reading to her: *Goodnight Moon, The Cat in the Hat, The Little Engine That Could, Charlotte's Web,* children's Bible stories (just as Mary Lou would sing to her "You Are My Sunshine," with the perfect pitch that had prompted Pete to tell his wife that she should join the church choir). That he would assure her that *The Legend of Sleepy Hollow* with its headless horseman was just a tale, she didn't need to have nightmares anymore. That he would show her how to hit and catch a softball. That he would push her on the swings at the playground at Clayton Avenue as she screamed "higher, daddy, higher" through her missing baby teeth. That he would take her to pick out and chop down a Christmas tree on the hill behind the home of friends of his parents. That he would come for her when just after her third birthday Mary Lou's sister Sally Rae Olsen volunteered to take Maddie so that she could play with cousin Christie, while Mary Lou dealt with a miscarriage. That when the plan backfired and Maddie became so despondent that she refused to eat or talk and Sally Rae telephoned from the trailer park in Chenango Bridge and said "she is miserable, please take her back," Pete would jump into the car and make the trip from Newburgh, where the three of them were living, in record time. That peering at her in the rearview mirror on the ride back, sick with worry, he would fret at the near-catatonic state homesickness had provoked in her and vow anew to keep her safe.

Maddie hated the resentment toward her father she felt as she walked from Farrar St. onto Grafton St. From there she would cut through the CVS parking lot to Massasoit Road and then head up Heywood St. toward St. V's Hospital and on down the long incline and through Kelley Square to Madison St. where her coach, if not her knight in shining armor, awaited; exactly as Julia Cruz had said she should.

Maddie was not your typical rebellious teenager. Far from it. She was the conformist who had collected Cabbage Patch dolls and read Judy Blume books, who never threw the DJ-like tantrums that struck such alarm in Pete and Mary Lou as they watched him hurl and suspend himself in the air, hang parallel to the floor for a second and then crash with a thud. She was the one who seldom talked back to her parents.

Defiance was out of character for her.

Still, she thought, *was there not just cause for holding what her father had done against him? To bolt? The insensitivity and unfairness of it! Erasing from my life everything that meant anything to me!* She thought of her bedroom with all of the girlish touches she had incorporated into it. Sunday mornings at church in the eleventh pew from the front on the right side of the sanctuary with sun streaming in through the stained-glass windows. Dinner afterwards at Gram Jenkins's home a block away. Aunts, uncles and cousins seated around the large antique bird's-eye maple dining room table, or everyone gathered at the picnic table in Pa Jenkins's open-sided shed out back, Pa firing up the grill with a gas line he'd run from the garage. Apple and strawberry picking in Pennsylvania. Visits with Grampa and Grandma Nash in the country where whiffle ball games were to the Nash's in their large yard what pickup touch football games were to the Kennedy's in Hyannis Port. Assembling complicated jigsaw puzzles with Grandma Nash. Swimming in the Clayton Ave. pool. Piano lessons. Front Street Days. Fourth of July fireworks. The Carvel ice cream store. Overnights with cousin Christie, with whom Maddie felt a particular rapport.

Then there was Jay Matthews, the boyfriend Maddie was leaving behind.

This, the unkindest cut of all—inflicted by Pete Nash

Junior Sanchez and three of his "bros" were tooling the streets of Vernon Hill in a battered black 1978 Ford Taurus. They were swigging from a bottle of cheap wine they had bought at Kirsch Liquors, passing it between themselves as they killed time until hooking up with a guy from Lowell Junior knew named Freddie Santiago. The meet would take place in the parking lot of the Worcester Senior Center on Providence St., as other rendezvous had in the past. Junior had chosen the location knowing that Worcester cops in their white patrol cars paid little mind to it after it had emptied out in late afternoon.

Sure the Taurus and Freddie's forest green Chevy Camaro would stick out even hidden as far from the street as possible. But the exchange would be over in less than a minute. Junior would have his bag of coke and Freddie would have his money and be on I-290 headed east toward Marlborough and then north on I-495.

Maddie was partway up Heywood St. on the steep climb toward St. V's, her legs feeling the strain of the ascent, her emotions a mix of regret about deserting her brother and sister to their fate, striking back at her father for forcing her into this rash retaliation and anticipating the reunion she would enjoy with Jay Matthews. From the hospital she would have an easier walk down to Kelley Square and through that befuddling intersection of six streets to Madison St.

Julia Cruz had told her the bus depot would be straight ahead, on her left.

How lost and alone she felt!

Maddie was unaware of the four men, all members of Worcester's notorious Latin Kings, when Junior from behind the steering wheel said to the others in the car as they swung a right onto Winthrop St. from Providence St., "yo, man, we need, like, bread. Funds are depleted, man!"

The transaction with Freddie Santiago had cost him a bundle.

At seventeen Junior was only two years older than Maddie but he might well have been from another planet with his ear and nose rings, neck and arm tattoos, goatee and jet-black hair pulled back and cinched in a pony tail. A faint, squiggly scar ran the length of his face from the edge of his left eye to his chin. It was a remnant of a skirmish he was proud of. The dude who'd given it to him when they tangled outside the Boys & Girls Club on Ionic Ave. had suffered worse. Junior had put him in St. V's with broken ribs and a broken shoulder.

Lean, mean and cocky, Junior was the scourge of Endicott St. from the third floor of his triple decker. He was an only child. He had aced his initiation with the gang that ruled Worcester's Main South by robbing the Dollar General store in broad daylight. He'd gotten away with a couple of hundred dollars and avoided being arrested. The Latin Kings liked his bravado and his style. He was ready to go to war with the Vice Lords if it came to that.

The Taurus' headlights beamed against the blue-and-white façade of St. V's as Junior guided the car around the corner nice and easy, his coal-black eyes attentive for any sign of the police. He was bouncing to the beat of LL Cool J's "Rock The Bells," the Hip Hop tune the opening lines of which he had altered to let everyone know he wasn't to be messed with. Now it went

Junior is hard as hell
Battle anybody I don't care who you tell
I excel, they all fail
I'm gonna crack shells, Junior must rock the bells

Junior in the Taurus was inching along Winthrop St. in front of the hospital, dishing jive and pondering where to go next. The night was young and his janitor father was probably drinking seventy five-cent drafts at the Hotel Vernon. Then he spotted Maddie. He slowed the Taurus so that it was hardly moving, his foot on the brake, his eyes taking in the sight of the girl walking by herself at 9:45 at night. A white girl in a hooded sweatshirt.

Junior brought the Taurus to a stop. He opened the window on the driver's side.

"Yo, wuz'up," he said.

Maddie could feel her heart skip a beat. She refused to acknowledge the greeting or to look toward where the voice came from. *Why, daddy, why* she thought, bemoaning, as she had repeatedly, her father's disregard for her welfare—so uncharacteristic of him. Suddenly her vulnerability became painfully apparent. She asked herself *what am I doing here? I wish I could snap my fingers, like Dorothy, and be in my rightful home again."*

Julia had warned her. "You be going through a tough neighborhood, Vernon Hill," she had said. "You got to keep moving. Don't stop for nobody, girl."

Maddie could feel Junior's eyes on her. As a fish out of water flops and squirms in sensing its doom, she was overcome by a realization that she was prey. She loathed the thought of what her stalkers might be up to.

She hastened her step, questioning now why she had set out on such a crazy mission, wondering if her father had discovered her absence and was maybe searching for her. Hoping that Pete would show up and she would climb into the Le Baron and be carted back to Cohasset St. and be glad she had.

Maddie heard the wheels of the Taurus scrunch on the street as it moved away from her. Her breathing came easier. She kept walking, her head down, her eyes fixed on the sidewalk, her heart pounding.

Suddenly Junior made a U-turn at Granite St.

Maddie didn't have to glance to her side to know that he was following her again. The Taurus crawled, hardly moving, Junior taking it all in.

She had never felt so helpless.

She quickened her pace.

Junior pulled the Taurus to a stop along the curb.

He got out of the car, waited, his body swaying to LL Cool J's snappy lines, the cats with him hooting and hollering in approval of his intentions—whatever they might be.

Maddie saw the lights of the Taurus out of the corner of her eye. She hurried to get past it.

The street appeared to be utterly desolate except for her, the Taurus, and its occupants.

"Where ya going, baby doll?"

Maddie looked up.

Junior was standing in front of her, blocking her path.

She froze.

In the distance she heard the faint blast of a siren.

CHAPTER TWO

DJ, IN THE THROES OF THE BEASTS OF THE WILD

July 1990

When they left DJ at the banks of the Androscoggin River he was standing in a group gathered in a large circle with his hands clasped into those of kindred spirits, most of them not old enough to vote but all of them wise enough in the art of creating mischief to be certifiable as juvenile delinquents.

Sprinkled amid this throng, which numbered about thirty persons in total, were half a dozen older individuals, male and female—clad in L.L. Bean boots, khaki shorts and yellow short-sleeved Polo shirts—monogrammed. They were holding clipboards. Whistles dangled from cords hung around their necks. They reminded Pete of the coaches DJ had answered to during midgets-league drills the Baby Bears had been put through at Arnold Park in Vestal, weeknights before their Saturday-morning games.

"How long ago that seems, given all that has transpired over the past five years," Pete thought.

"DJ was a mere innocent then."

Pete and Mary Lou were sitting in their car along the road, ready to pull away from rural Maine, eager to turn DJ over to a program that was fashioned specifically for troubled teens and that would keep him under wraps for thirty days. Pete had read about it in a magazine. He had been intrigued by the possibility that a month in the wilderness could straighten DJ out. His own patience was wearing thin. He did not know what it would take to save his son.

Desperation being the mother of invention, and with Mary Lou in agreement, he had written out a check for three thousand five hundred fifty dollars and no cents, in the name of Outward Bound's "Hurricane Island Land Program."

In contemplating the scene, Pete tried to suppress the notion that he had been guilty of a serious miscalculation in trading up for a better job; for discarding Binghamton in favor of Boston. He didn't want to admit that he might have been wrong even though the evidence in affirmation of this fact was mounting.

His mind fell back to those practices at Arnold Park, high above the center of town on a blustery hill, how he would bring coffee with him in a Styrofoam cup and sit atop a picnic table with his feet on the bench seat and watch as DJ and his little teammates learned the basics of blocking and tackling and running plays; this beneath a setting sun. Pete would pull his windbreaker tight around him while conversing with other parents and savoring the sound of bodies banging and crashing. As a sportswriter at the time, his ears were accustomed to the thump of the hits, even from press boxes a fair distance from the playing field. He could picture DJ suiting up for Coach Hoover, the coach in his ever-present trench coat, watching implacably from the sidelines as DJ sprang forward from his position at free safety to cut the heels from under a running back.

DJ weighed just sixty-five pounds then, fully suited and fully geared up at kickoff with knee and shoulder pads and spikes on his feet and a helmet on his head. He was your typical Vestal small fry but with an appetite for the fray and so he would plunge into the mayhem and come away grass and mud-stained and Mary Lou would have to give his uniform an extra dose of Tide to get it white again.

The Baby Bears finished that season undefeated. DJ's love of sport, as strong as that of his father, was set. Playing with Tonka trucks, playing in the sandbox, riding his Big Wheels and spending hour after hour with his Lincoln logs, Slinky and Rubik's cube gave way to an infatuation with the National Pastime, the NFL and the NBA. As his father had before him, he started a baseball card collection. Pete would purchase a pack of Topps baseball cards every time DJ hit a home run with the whiffle ball bat in the yard behind the house, DJ shouting "it's gone!" as the ball began its trajectory toward the spruce trees at the rear of the property.

Now, six months past his fourteenth birthday, DJ was stretching out to his eventual height of six-foot-one. He would ultimately weigh two hundred thirty pounds with strong forearms and wrists, and be able to yank the yucca plants that Pete despised out of the ground by the roots with his bare hands. He would also be able to hoist a barrel of yard debris onto his shoulders and carry it to be dumped into the bed of a pickup truck.

At fourteen, though, he was downright scrawny. With a final glance at the group next to the river before starting the four-hour drive back to Northbridge, Pete easily picked DJ out by his long hair.

"At Parris Island, twenty-five years ago, they shaved mine off in less than a minute after I got off the bus," Pete mused.

Pete hesitated. He was having second thoughts.

Mary Lou was crying.

"Are you sure we are doing the right thing?" she asked.

"Yes," Pete said.

"No.

"Maybe."

II

Any number of provocations had brought them to this point.

Pete recalled being awakened at midnight by the ring of the front doorbell on Cohasset St. Mary Lou wouldn't have heard it; she suffered from bone deafness in both ears and put her hearing aids away in the nightstand before turning out the light each night. A Worcester cop was saying "he was drinking from an open container over on Hamilton St., outside Husson's Market. He can't be doing that, sir." Pete thanked the officer, closed the heavy door, heard it click shut and, with rage filling his chest, slapped DJ hard across the cheek. He regretted hitting him the instant DJ's flesh turned pink, just as he would lament berating him verbally countless times afterwards, when his frustration boiled over.

By this time DJ was running with several ruffians who had grown up on the unforgiving streets of Worcester. One of them, Thomas Jankowski, the son of a barber who had a shop in nearby Rice Square, had appointed himself DJ's protector. Compassion prompted Thomas Jankowski to hold DJ's would-be tormentors at bay.

Tommy had first noticed DJ being harassed at Dartmouth Street Elementary when both were fifth graders. "Mess with him and you answer to me," he had told the assailant, who quickly backed off. The bully knew that Tommy's physicality had been honed by slugfests with his older brother John in the three-decker home on Plantation St. in which the entire Jankowski clan lived (on separate floors by generation, as was the local custom). What he couldn't understand was why Tommy would come to the defense of an outsider, a softie with a strange accent who practically begged to be beaten on.

With his concern for the underdog Tommy had brought DJ into the fold, accepting him as an equal with Travis Nolan and Jerry Conrad. DJ was not in their league for toughness—a required commodity in Worcester as it was in Lowell and Lawrence and Fall River. But he relished being part of Tommy's crew. Together the four of them congregated afternoons at the Jankowski home where DJ was treated with kid gloves by Tommy's parents and grandmother over plates heaped with Polish sausage, boiled potatoes and carrots. The four of them drank and smoked weed and hung out at the Worcester Common Outlets and at a makeshift fort they built from scrap material on Crow Hill. They laughed in the face of the teachers at East Middle, DJ all the while drifting steadily into a deeper attachment to alcohol which he saw as a buffer against the feeling of inferiority that nagged at him. He would adopt a routine as class clown that would serve his need to be popular in school in Worcester, and then in Northbridge after Pete and Mary Lou decided that a community similar demographically to Vestal might be just what was needed to rescue Donald Jeremiah and Katherine Rose from the turbulence that governed life at Worcester East Middle.

Pete would learn that DJ had taken his first sip of beer before the move to Massachusetts. He couldn't help himself. He was worried about Pete. Throughout the summer of '85, as Mary Lou tried to sell the house in Vestal, Pete had been commuting to and from Massachusetts on a motorcycle. One Friday night he pulled in later than usual, his right elbow and right knee bloodied. He had lost control of the handlebars of the motorcycle on the Massachusetts Turnpike in an attempt to get back on the highway from the shoulder of the road after stopping beneath an overpass in a flash storm to change into his rain suit. DJ had watched in his pajamas as Mary Lou nursed Pete's scrapes. When his parents went to bed, he crept down the stairs and took one of Pete's Bass Ales from the refrigerator.

The way DJ saw it, Pete had deserted him.

It was no different now in Massachusetts.

"Dad, he's never around," DJ thought. How he wanted his father back. But Pete's time was owned by Fred and Judith Phelps at the newspaper office on Harvard St. in Brookline. It had been that way since Pete told Mary Lou he would be accepting the position of editor with Citizen Inc.

DJ could not understand what would compel his father to abandon the family for a job so far away. He could not bring himself to appreciate that Pete came home to him most every weekend despite Phelps' insistence that he stay in Boston to soak up the atmosphere of the city, make himself visible and promote the Phelps's group of weeklies.

He only knew that he feared for what this change meant.

So DJ had turned to the beer his father drank on the couch while watching the Knicks, Giants or Yankees.

He guzzled it down.

The buzz it gave him alleviated some of the hurt.

AS PETE shifted from park to drive he knew that DJ was where he needed to be. In the ensuing weeks DJ would write him letters filled with remorse for his misdeeds and promising to reform himself. He would stuff these into an envelope that smelled of pine needles and the out of doors, that was smudged with dirt and hastily and crookedly sealed. In these, in a scrawl and with many of the words misspelled—as befit the struggle he was having trying to learn the lessons he was being taught in school—DJ talked of the beauty of the Maine woods in a manner that reminded Pete that he was his mother's son. Like Mary Lou, DJ was enthralled with Nature in all of its manifestations. Like Mary Lou, he was known to wax poetic about sunsets and rainbows and a harvest moon and eclipses and rhododendrons in springtime and rabbits and deer and the kind of quirky cloud formations that spoke wonders to him.

My counselors are grate, dad! (he wrote). *I met a girl! Her name is Jodie. From Waltham. We have a lot in common. She likes Led Zeppelin and Ozzie! She plays hacky sack! I like her a lot. We are kep busy. You are not gonna believe it but I am going to be doin a three-day solo. Just me in a tent. I'm scard about that. Oh, I saw a moose!"*

Reading these letters, which he put in a drawer of his desk as they accumulated, Pete felt hope for an outcome that would dull the pain of the shocking loss of Maddie—five years earlier. Losing two of his children to "The Move" was unthinkable (the wide rectangular billboard along the Mass Pike in Allston that he passed each morning, with pictures of missing children, reminded Pete of the tragedy his family had suffered). DJ, he knew, was in an even more precarious spot than Maddie had been. "Being thrashed to a pulp by half the town" in Worcester, as put it, and then in Northbridge, had plunged him deeper into a reliance on booze. He drank incessantly, stashing Bud Light empties wherever he thought Pete might not find them and yet they turned up, tucked into a corner of DJ's closet, under his bed or beneath a pile of leaves in the yard. They were scattered inside and outside the house, not obvious like Post-it notes but with the same intended effect. It was DJ's way of saying to Pete *you did this, I haven't forgotten the anguish you've caused.* Pete knew too that his son's disillusionment with him was more profound than Maddie's had been. He wasted no chance to throw in his father's face the damage that had been perpetrated by Pete's arbitrary and inconsiderate step.

Pete detected in the letters from the White Mountains, however, none of the boy's usual persistent reminders that he had screwed up as a father. Instead DJ wrote expansively and poignantly about the joy he was experiencing in roughing it. *Like when cousin Myles let me and Kate follow him and his dog Patches when they went into the forest behind Gram Nash's house. Myles would climb trees and swing from branches like Tarzan and he took us to this amazing waterfall. We'd be gone for hours. Remember, dad?*

The last letter Pete received from DJ was dated July 23, 1990. Pete and Mary Lou were planning to pick him up the following Saturday and treat him to dinner and then shopping at the Kittery Outlets on the way home.

Dad, I cant stand it. All alone out here far from base camp, rain, wind, thunder and lightning and its pitch dark ive never been so afraid! Im on Day 3 and im almost done and im tryin to stay strong so I can see you and ma and tell you all about it.

Pete laid the letter on the table next to the recliner and turned off the lamp.

He dozed off.

In his tent DJ prayed. Above him the heavens crackled. He covered his ears against the incessant booms, which seemed to shake the whole hillside. The flashes of light—bright and menacing—smothered him. Jarred him. He remembered Pete telling him about the time he and Maddie were sitting on the patio behind the house on Hoffman Avenue, about to go inside as a storm broke, when a bolt struck the O'Brien's tree, next door. "It shredded the bark clean off the trunk for twenty feet from the ground up," Pete had said. "I could feel the vibration in my toes. I could smell it, the burnt bark."

DJ crawled into his sleeping bag, trying to blot out the thoughts of the savagery of remote Maine in the blazing heat of summertime.

"Jesus," he said, "let there be an Outward Bound counselor keeping an eye on me like they said they would. They said we wouldn't be stranded. They said they'd be close by even if we couldn't see them."

Forty yards away, six wolves, the gray of their shaggy coats lying flat on their soaked skin, their yellow eyes gleaming, moved in unison toward the tent.

Pete awoke, overcome by a sudden certainty that DJ's life was at risk.

"Something's very wrong," he thought.

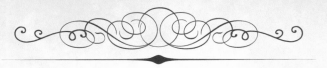

CHAPTER THREE

Kate, offering assurance: I'm fine, pops'

September 2018

Kate at forty-three retained all of the ebullience that had marked her personality from a young age. Much had changed, however. Now, although still effervescent, engaging and indomitable, a complete extrovert—which had made her popular in social engagements and which had prompted Pete to dub her "Kiss-Me-Kate"—she was in crisis.

Pete had always thought of Katherine Rose as the likeliest of he and Mary Lou's three children to emerge from any difficulty unscathed; that she would be okay "Crossing Muddy Waters" as John Hiatt would have said, and did, in song.

The same independent streak and yearning for thrills that had compelled her, when she was no bigger than a mouse at five and six, to submit to an instinct to wander from the house in Vestal, leaving Pete and Mary Lou distraught as to her whereabouts and triggering a desperate canvassing of the neighborhood, had also carried her through a series of tumultuous relationships. One of these had resulted in the birth of her daughter Evelyn with a moody and unstable prospective husband who was the product of a broken marriage.

Kate was living with Josh Cannon in a house that had been in his family for years, in a neighboring town, when he appeared to self-destruct. They had been planning their nuptials. Instead he fled to Florida. One minute Pete was accompanying Kate to the Myriad Ballroom and the Cocke 'n Kettle to inquire about the costs of a wedding ceremony and the next Josh was fifteen hundred miles away, wrestling not with alligators but with the demons that had pushed him to the precipice of a mental breakdown.

Only a self-professed dependence on marijuana seemed to help.

Before Josh there had been Kevin Lane, a rascal and a rogue. After Josh there had been Jeb and Lou and Stan and Doug and finally Frank.

The common thread in Kate's life beginning almost simultaneously with Pete's initiation of The Move, besides an ever-present man, was alcohol. Just a year and ten days younger than DJ, she, like her big brother, had fallen victim to its allure. She and DJ had done their best to cope in the cauldron they perceived Worcester to be. They had even at Pete's suggestion taken on paper routes, delivering the afternoon editions and the Sunday issue of the *Telegram & Gazette* to the three-decker homes that lined Ingleside and Farrar and Dana and reveling in the pocket money that this work brought. With Tommy Jankowski and his pals they had also found the refuge they were looking for, except that it came with a price. Tommy would shield them from threats to their well-being. They in turn would partake in the mind-bending intoxicants that were part of being "with Tommy." Boosts of this sort were the cost of membership, not just in Tommy's clan but in most other similar couplings in the city.

II

Pete was a pushover where his youngest daughter was concerned, which is why he sprang to her assistance when she and Frank Valentine's co-habitation in a second-story apartment in Northbridge—just three miles from he and Mary Lou's own home—disintegrated. He had understood for some time that Kate's need for a man was as great as her need for the small pink blanket she called her "ya ya," which accompanied her wherever she went and that she still insisted on throwing over herself at night even though it was falling apart.

Among Pete's many laments in assessing Kate's current difficulties as a repercussion of The Move had been sectioning her in Uxbridge District Court. This came two men before she fell in with the man she invariably called by his full given name of "Frank Allen Valentine." She had identified all of her boyfriends, "Stanley Livingston Fellows" and the others, this way. It was a compulsion of hers that Pete found endearing.

Frank and Stanley were both employed by a company in Grafton that manufactured freestanding displays for the lobbies of banks, high-end coffee shops and corporate offices, even for the new ballpark in the Twin Cities of Minnesota. "The Dunlap Boys," Kate had christened them. They were heavy drinkers on the job and off. Their allegiance to John Dunlap was exceeded only by their proficiency with specialty saws and other machinery they used to build out the promotional paraphernalia that had made John Dunlap a millionaire.

The deterioration of the bond between Kate and Stanley was hastened by the twenty-four packs of Miller Lite the The Dunlap Boys consumed while pitching pennies, tossing horseshoes, playing "corn hole" or just sitting around a fire in lawn chairs. Kate fully embraced this lifestyle. The minute it dissolved, she was rudderless.

When she and Stanley and Evelyn were rousted from their apartment by a fire that started in the basement of the two-family home they were occupying, the couple split and Kate and Evelyn moved in once again with Pete and Mary Lou. Evelyn had spent most of her formative years with her grandparents. The arrangement this time lasted only until Kate's drinking got out of hand. Pete had no recourse but to go before a judge and have her committed to the Women's Addiction Treatment Center (WAT-C) in Fall River.

Jess Cannon, Josh's sister, took temporary custody of Evelyn. Evelyn, by then in high school, was so irate over her parents' conduct that she pushed them aside. Worse, her estrangement soon seemed to extend to Pete and Mary Lou, for reasons they could not understand.

"She has turned her back on her grandparents. Another penance I must deal with for my blind pursuit of personal ambition," Pete thought.

"Promise me you will never do that to me again, dad!" Kate had said, on the ride back to Northbridge from Fall River. She had thrived in the program there. Lingering, however, was resentment at the treatment she had been subjected to. "The police shackled me and kept me in the holding cell overnight. I have never been so humiliated!" she said.

Pete could feel his heart shatter, hearing this.

Kate and DJ's friend Daryl Nichols had accompanied Pete and Mary Lou on the short trip to Massachusetts's South Coast. Daryl was the divorced father of three boys, a sometime body builder, sometime guitar player and musician, sometime hunter and sometime teller of tall tales whose infatuation with Kate had led him to take her on as a rehabilitation project.

"I am going to marry that girl," Daryl had said, on the ride. Pete believed him. Pete considered Daryl to be almost a second son. He was with Bert Wallace, Phil Parker and DJ one of "The Four Amigos" in Northbridge. They would traipse into Pete and Mary Lou's home and begin chowing through the milk and orange juice and pasta and cookies and ice cream before heading up to DJ's bedroom to play Nintendo or listen to AC/DC.

Daryl was not only DJ's best friend, he was enamored with Kate.

Kate moved in with Daryl, Daryl's sister Sherri and her husband and Daryl's mother Angelina.

A few nights later, Kate began drinking again.

On Friday night of that first week, sneaking away to buy nips, she tripped and fell.

Daryl texted Pete.

I'm done. She won't even try to stay sober.

III

In replacing Stanley Livingston Fellows with Frank Allen Valentine, Kate maintained her connection with The Dunlap Boys and their goings-on. "Doesn't this just make perfect sense," Pete told himself. "Maddie's life claimed by a ruthless city, DJ's by wild animals. Now Kate's deteriorating health, exacerbated by heavy drinking."

Pete liked Frank Valentine to the extent that it was possible. He tried to overlook Frank's addiction to beer, which he swilled morning, noon and night. He chain smoked too. Pete was sure this combination would amount to a death sentence for Frank, whose spare frame, accented by a shallow face and a bug-eyed dubiousness of people he didn't know, suggested a heart attack waiting to happen. He was after all in his late forties, a prime age for such a calamity. Pete's greater concern was that Frank wasn't all in with Kate; or with he and Mary Lou. He was at ease with The Dunlap Boys, but detached in his infrequent contact with the two of them. The nickname of "Meatball" he had attached to Kate was seen by her as a symbol of his fondness for her. Pete saw it, however, as demeaning.

The abrupt demise of Dunlap Display Co. after the death of John Dunlap sent Frank into a tailspin. Within months Dunlap's widow Tran had mismanaged the company into near-insolvency. Dunlap Display was reeling. "She hasn't been paying my health insurance!" Frank told Kate, as Stanley before him had. "How can she get away with *that*?"

With the end of Dunlap Display in 2017, Frank put in for unemployment. His weeks out of work piled up. As they did, and his reliance on booze to fill his empty hours increased, Kate's assertions that he needed to find a job proved futile. Frank threw back at her that she wasn't working either. Pete had seen this scenario play out before. He had always wanted to believe that Kate's rotten luck with men would eventually improve; that she and Frank would be the love story he desired for her. He knew, however, that it was unlikely. Alcohol was the spoiler. Now Frank and Kate were both drinking around the clock.

The problem was that Pete had a blind spot where Kate was concerned. He tended to see only her many winning attributes, not her flaws. Her inherently positive disposition, her likeability, her intelligence, her mastery of any task she undertook including cooking, cleaning and computers, her strength when facing adversity and her devotion to family including her nieces and nephew were what convinced him that Kate was worth his effort.

So intense was Pete's conviction that Kate would straighten out that he tolerated her weakness. He would do anything to help her, even if it meant unwittingly enabling the addiction that was the source of all her troubles. She would con him into transporting her to the liquor store to cash in returns and come back not only with a pack of cigarettes but whiskey in her purse.

Kate played him for a sucker.

She had been doing exactly that for a long time.

IV

Pete and Kate were crossing the parking lot toward the Dollar Tree store in Northbridge when she said to him "it's pretty pathetic when a daughter has to ask her father to buy personal hygiene items for her."

Her remark struck a nerve. "Believe me, daughter, that's not the most pathetic thing about all of this."

He wanted her to think about what she was doing to him. The trips to Walmart, Pete putting on his credit card various must-haves that Kate had requested: dishwashing liquid, paper towels, toilet paper, bread, milk, peanut butter, a box of pasta, a jar of olives. These he didn't object to. Nor did he mind bringing her a week's worth of the newspaper so that she could read it in bed.

None of this provoked in him a sense that he was being manipulated; used.

He bristled, however, when Kate's demands became more of an imposition as Frank removed himself of the responsibility of providing for her. When Frank's daughter and two infant sons moved in with them as relief from threats Vanessa Valentine was receiving from her boyfriend, it was suddenly five people in a tiny apartment. Tensions were stretched to the snapping point. "I promise it won't be for long," Vanessa told Frank. She had taken out a restraining order on Lance Andrews, the father of her children. He was suffering from PTSD after serving in Iraq.

Things went from bad to worse. Frank spent most of the day in the hallway outside the apartment except when he was watching the Bruins on TV, perched on a stool, drinking, keeping a wary eye on the street from beneath the tip of his John Deere cap. Coming and going, Pete thought it the strangest thing he had ever seen, Frank nodding a hello, Pete responding in kind.

Frank's car was repossessed. The utility bills went unpaid. So did the rent. The landlord raised the specter of eviction. Arguments ensued.

One day Kate decided to accompany Pete and Mary Lou to Hampton Beach.

When she returned, Frank was gone.

He left the furniture behind.

V

Without Frank and with Vanessa and the boys out too, Kate was on her own. Winter came. Spring. The buds on the magnolia in front of Pete and Mary Lou's house flowered in a burst of white petals, awakening in the neighborhood a conviction that all was right with the world.

Pete was sure, however, that this was not the case.

Kate and Pete talked every day and he would come by in the afternoon to take out her trash and she would join him for a walk up and down the streets around her apartment. Pete noticed that she was frailer; and weaker. "You're not eating enough," he said. "It's got to be more than slices of salami and American cheese and Mt. Olive pickles. Your arms and legs are too skinny. Mom will send you some leftovers."

"I'm fine, pops," Kate said, laboring for breath in her size five sneakers as she tried to keep up with him. "You're always saying I don't weigh enough. You know I don't want to be fat."

With that Pete's mind flashed back to '89 and how close he had come to seeing Kate snatched from he and Mary Lou's grasp. DJ too. The two of them had fallen under the hypnotic spell of one Kevin Lane shortly after the family's relocation from Worcester to Northbridge. The incident still haunted Pete. The damage the Lane boy caused left a wound that had never healed. It still festered and oozed even after Lane was sentenced to fifteen years in federal prison for using drug money to bankroll two restaurants he owned in Worcester—long afterwards.

Kate had met Lane at a muddy space next to the Blackstone River on the northeast side of town, where kids she and DJ's age gathered to drink and smoke on Saturday nights when they were supposed to be roller skating at the community center. The spot was called "Pipeline" because of the concrete cylinders on the far side of the river that carried waste to the sewage treatment plant two miles away. Pete and Mary Lou were naïve enough to think that DJ and Kate were where they said they'd be.

As a moth is drawn to flame, Kate was lured by his particular magnetism to Kevin Lane, in cozying up to him at the bonfire around which a dozen or so high schoolers congregated until being rousted by the Northbridge PD. No one was ever arrested, they were simply told "you're trespassing on Rod & Gun Club land, clear on out of here, boys and girls."

Long-haired, flippant, defiant of adult authority and incorrigible to the tips of his toes, Lane had already attracted a small entourage, Charles Manson-like, when DJ and Kate spun their way into his orbit. DJ saw Lane as a suitable replacement in Northbridge for Tommy Jankowski in Worcester. He did not see Lane's proclivity for acts of disobedience and petty thievery as a disqualifier but as the mark of a born leader. Kate saw Lane as the dominant male influence she craved.

Destiny took its course. The more DJ and Kate floundered in trying to acclimate themselves to high school in Northbridge, the easier it became for them to bend to Kevin Lane's will.

Pete did not initially see Lane as a threat. But with each day that passed and DJ and Kate's infatuation with him increasing by the hour, Pete's anxiety grew.

By now Pete had gotten used to telling himself "it's one dilemma and one setback after another, for us."

Kevin Lane would prove to be all the Nash family could handle.

VI

Pete and Mary Lou had not lost Maddie. Worcester had not snatched her up. In the uncertainty of the moment, in the fear that gripped him after he discovered that she had walked away with little regard for what might happen to her, Pete had simply imagined such an outcome, as a worse-case scenario.

Neither had DJ been sacrificed to the ferociousness of the untamed wilderness in Maine. Pete had dreamt of his son's demise before waking from a nap and telling himself "pull it together. He is alright. He will be home soon."

Having seen DJ and Kate almost assimilated into a band of teenage desperadoes and forever turning their backs on he and Mary Lou even before their struggles escalated over the years that followed should have been all the warning Pete needed to know that the family's ordeal was just beginning.

His assertion to DJ and Kate that he was ending their contact with Kevin Lane blew up in his face. He was not prepared for what brother and sister decided should be their response to his order that they terminate the relationship.

"DJ and Kate are gone," he said to Mary Lou, one morning. "They must have left during the night."

For weeks until then, Pete, Mary Lou, Maddie, DJ and Kate had been in consultation with a counselor at a family crisis resolution center in Milford, in an attempt to sort out the "who, what, why, when, where and how" of their ordeal. They all laughed in noticing, the first time they went there, that the facility was located on "Asylum Drive," just up the road from Milford Regional Hospital.

The name on the street sign suggested to them a "we're-not-crazy-yet-here-we-are-anyway" kind of acknowledgement of their predicament. With it, too, a hope that talking things out would bring them back together, as they took seats on chairs and a sofa across from Jeanne Nguyen in a dimly lit room with the drapes drawn and the door closed and waited for her to start the conversation. This occurred weekly.

Ms. Nguyen was a pert, dark-haired woman, no older than her mid-forties (Pete guessed), fashionably dressed and cheerful. She encouraged each of them to express their feelings openly and honestly. Studying her as she coaxed and prodded them, Pete looked upon her as an angelic presence. "She makes no effort to cast aspersions," he thought. "She puts all of her energy into keeping us on subject. I like her."

At first, the charges flew so fast that Pete barely had time to respond. "They are ganging up on me," he thought. "I guess they have every right. I am the reason Mary Lou is so discouraged, Maddie is so disillusioned, DJ and Kate so alienated. I never should have made them surrender the life they knew in Vestal to my desire for one that is just the opposite of what they had there." He nevertheless resented being made to shoulder such guilt. He didn't like being constantly on the defensive. He wondered why Jeanne Nguyen didn't raise a finger to stop the assault.

The second or third week, Pete lifted Kevin Lane up as the root of all evil and the instigator of all of their current difficulties.

"He stole them from us," Pete said. "We had no idea where they were. It was frightening. One night, after dark, I caught a glimpse of Kate walking up the street from our house. She had thrown a rock through the pane of glass next to the front door! She escaped into a wooded area. Our neighbor Mike Gosselin agreed to help me search for them. Thank God for Mike. He's got a generous heart. He is adored by all, especially children.

"One morning, it must have been the fourth or fifth day after they had left, Mike and I were over by the Catholic church on Linwood Street, about a half mile from our house, when he pointed and said 'maybe there, that garage apartment set back from the road. It looks empty. The perfect hiding place.'

"At the end of a dirt driveway we climbed some steps as quietly as possible and opened the door. There they were, half a dozen of them sprawled around with not a care in the world, empty beer cans on the kitchen counter, cigarette butts everywhere.

"I told DJ and Kate that they were squatting. 'It's illegal. You have to come home.' I put an end to the Kevin Lane business right then and there.

"But that only drove a bigger wedge between us."

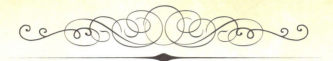

CHAPTER FOUR

KATHERINE ROSE, AT DEATH'S DOOR

It all came back to the job in Brookline never having been meant to succeed. It was apparent to Pete that despite the experience he had gained as news editor of a large daily and Sunday newspaper in Binghamton, he was no better equipped to guide the fortunes of an upstart company like Citizen Inc. for Fred and Judith Phelps, in competition with the *Boston Globe*, the *Boston Herald* and the *Boston Phoenix*, than Maddie had been in facing the bestiality of Worcester or DJ had been in trying to cope with the ridicule he faced at Dartmouth Street School and Worcester East Middle and then the brutality of the Maine woods.

Pete had walked away from Citizen Inc. after receiving a "shape up or ship out" note from Fred Phelps in the summer of 1988. "It's amazing I lasted two and a half years," he thought, as he read Phelps's handwritten communication in his small office at the back of the newsroom on a Friday night. The next issue of *The Boston Ledger* had been put to bed. Pete's young staff writers and Citizen Inc.'s compositors had left the building. Phelps was not hovering as he often did.

Digesting Phelps's words, which were written on his personal stationary, with a caricature of Fred running like a sprinter across the top of the paper, Peter understood what he had to do. "This is an ultimatum," he thought. "There is no way I can measure up to his expectations. I have to bury my pride and leave."

Before penning his own message of farewell to his people, dropping the notes on their desks and heading west to Worcester, Pete considered what plans Fred must have already formulated for the "post-Pete Nash" era. That's when it occurred to him that "Fred's going to give my spot to Michael Goldman. It's been trending in that direction."

Fred had brought Goldman on as a contributing columnist. Goldman's assignment was to write articles on politics in the city. Politics was second only to the perpetual discussion of the ups and downs of the Red Sox as Bostonians' primary preoccupation. New England weather was a close third—and often first, when nor'easters barreled through, battering the coast and sending WBZ-TV and WNBC-TV reporters flocking to Nantasket Beach in Hull for eyewitness accounts of the havoc, the sea wall being pounded.

At first, Goldman befriended Pete. "I've got an extra bedroom at my place in Wayland you can use," he had said, when Pete mentioned that he was going to have to give up the room he was renting from a family on Commonwealth Avenue in Chestnut Hill, near Boston College. "I've only got it until the kids from BC come back in August," Pete had said.

Goldman took it upon himself to familiarize Pete with Boston. Pete was grateful. In his Saab, Goldman would chauffeur Pete to Filene's Basement, at Downtown Crossing; around the narrow streets of Beacon Hill ("there's the Public Garden, there's the State House, there's the Cheers bar, there's John Kerry's residence"); across the Tobin Bridge heading north to a bookstore in Winchester that Goldman frequented; over the Charles River to Harvard Square and lunch at the Charles Hotel; into the North End for a cannoli; into Charlestown for a peek at the creation of housing for Yuppies in the former Navy Yard, adjacent to *Old Ironsides*. All the while Goldman would keep up a running dialogue about the people and places and things that made Boston tick; that infused the Hub with a class that in his mind solidified its position as the world's most civilized and interesting city. Foremost, he told Pete, were the universities and the medical institutions. "It's why Boston is the Athens of America," Goldman said.

Sitting next to Goldman, Pete could picture him in his tweed jacket at the front of an amphitheater at Northeastern or Tufts, lecturing seventy students on the roles Ralph Waldo Emerson and Henry David Thoreau played in shaping the character of the Commonwealth. Or on the importance of John Adams, Paul Revere, Bunker Hill, the Boston Tea Party, the Boston Massacre, Lexington and Concord, Robert Frost and Harriet Beecher Stowe.

Pete had not hired Goldman. Fred had. But Pete understood that the columns Goldman wrote, addressing the political ramifications of decisions made by Mayor Ray Flynn and the Boston City Council (personified by the colorful language employed by the flamboyant Albert Leo "Dapper" O'Neil) on such boiling issues as rent control, gentrification, parking bans, traffic congestion, racial divisions and commercial development (which was threatening the stability of the South End, the Back Bay and Allston-Brighton), lent sorely needed credibility to The Citizen's handful of tabloids. Goldman knew the players. He knew the issues. He knew how to turn in copy that would sell newspapers.

Pete thought of Michael Goldman only as an asset, never as a liability to him. Because of the erudition that Goldman brought to his work, Pete could overlook his new friend's slobby living habits: half-eaten bowls of Wheaties sitting on the coffee table in the parlor, clothes strewn about as if a tornado had hit the house, mice scurrying across the kitchen counter, the bed that Goldman never bothered to make that was piled high with shirts and sport coats one of which he would grab on his way out the door. These irritations, though they grated on him, Pete dismissed as the oddities of an absent-minded professor.

He appreciated that Goldman for his part did not attempt to step between Pete and his writers. Even when he saw Goldman prepping them, coaching them, privately, in the center of the newsroom before they charged into action like knights-errant—like a Don Quixote on his trusty steed "Rozinante"—Pete surmised that he was just being helpful.

Now, in realizing the enormity of his situation, in anticipating what Mary Lou would say when he reached Grafton Hill unemployed ("what are you going to do now?"), Pete put the pieces together.

Michael Goldman had been seizing control of the newsroom.

Right under Pete's nose.

II

Alone in an otherwise empty apartment as the months on the calendar flipped from August to September to October, Kate settled in for the long haul. She refused to budge. She intended to stay until driven out. "This is the streak of stubbornness that has always defined her," Pete thought. "Despite her lack of height, she will not be pushed around." He thought of the many occasions on which Kate had stood up for herself. Good luck to bigger and stronger types—live-in male companions, former girlfriends with whom she'd had a falling out and who were now disparaging her on Facebook, or bill collectors—in trying to intimidate her into submitting to their dictates or threats. Pete had never known anyone who was an impervious to orders or reprimands, regardless of the consequences an obliviousness to them might bring, than Kate Nash.

"Where does this backbone come from?" he would ask himself. "Not from me. I'm a coward by comparison." He recalled the time he was pulled over on I-88 heading back to Worcester from Vestal by a state trooper who said to him when he rolled down the driver's-side window "I've been tailing you for some time, you're doing 80 in a 65, sir" and how he later related to members of the family that he had jokingly responded "well it took you a while to catch up, didn't it" when in fact he had said "sorry about that, officer."

Kate was the one with spunk. Sometimes, Pete thought, to her own detriment.

When Pete learned that Kate's landlord was suffering from cancer and not expected to live long, he said "this isn't right, taking advantage of those people by staying when you should leave. He's an assistant principal at the Christian school, isn't that what you said? I feel so bad for them."

Pete wondered how much protecting his own reputation in town had to do with it. His history as a newspaperman in Northbridge and Worcester was untarnished, Kate's as someone the NPD was familiar with as a result of run-ins they'd had with her—in association and apart from The Dunlap Boys—not so much. Thankfully, he often thought, her record with the NPD was clean.

"Again me, thinking of my self-interests," Pete thought.

A summons to housing court directed to Frank Allen Valentine arrived in the mail. Kate laid it aside. The landlord's wife tacked "when are you leaving?" notes on the door. The handwriting suggested ire. Kate removed them. The landlord's wife knocked on the door. Kate refused to let her in, insisting to Pete "I have rights."

"That's not the point. You're being unfair. They are owed some respect."

Pete knew that Kate was drinking with neighbors. He knew she was finding ways, without any income, to keep herself supplied with alcohol. He knew too that she was growing weaker by the day. Each time he came by he was shocked at the sight of the anorexic-like condition into which she'd slipped.

"You need to check into a program," he said. "AdCare in Worcester, Spectrum in Westborough. Somewhere."

"I will, dad,"

25

She promised to begin calling rehab facilities and she did.

Beds were scarce. "It's the opioid crisis," she said. "I'll keep trying."

III

The first time Kate needed a ride to the hospital, she went by ambulance.

The second time, she called Pete to drive her. She told him she'd been vomiting for hours. She couldn't even keep ice chips or water down. She was frail and shaky. He had to help her down the stairs to the street and into the car. She wrapped herself in her blanket to ward off the chills. She coughed and gagged and spit into a Styrofoam cup on the way to Milford.

Pete was feeling sorry for himself. "This is what it has come to for me at the age of seventy-three," he thought. "Will I never be past this obligation?"

At the top of the driveway leading to the brand-new, multimillion-dollar ER, an attendant noticed the difficulty Pete was having helping Kate out of the car. Together they got her into a wheelchair.

She was hospitalized for several days, put on an IV of Gatorade, subjected to a battery of tests, examined by a squadron of doctors, catered to by a half dozen nurses.

"Extreme dehydration" was finally fingered as the cause of her difficulties.

"I'll make an appointment with Dr. Dalrymple for follow-up," she told Pete.

Raymond Dalrymple was a legend in the Blackstone Valley of Massachusetts. People thought of him as a Dr. Kildare or a Dr. Welby with a bedside manner that was such a rich blend of conscientiousness and consideration that people stumbled over one another, clamoring for his services. Kate and Evelyn had both been seeing him since Evelyn was an infant. "Don't ever retire," Kate said to him.

Soft-spoken, with a cherubic face, pale blue eyes and hair that had gone as white as the lab coat he wore over his shirt and tie, he had been encouraging Kate to get her drinking under control for years.

"How long are we going to be fighting this battle?" he would ask her.

Pete knew Dr. Dalrymple from the good doctor's days as the Northbridge High football team's physician. They would patrol the sidelines behind the Rams' bench on Saturday afternoons, Dr. Dalrymple armed with the stethoscope that always hung around his neck and with low-cut cleats on his feet for traction if he needed to jog onto the field to tend to an injured player, Pete with the camera he always carried with him. They would exchange pleasantries back and forth.

Once, when Pete sliced his left forefinger with an Xacto knife in the middle of the night while pasting together an edition of the hometown newspaper he was rushing to print, Ray Dalrymple stitched him up in the morning.

"Sorry!" Dr. Dalrymple said, seeing Pete wince while he sulfurized the cut.

"Be done in a second."

The job was so neatly performed that it didn't even leave a scar.

Pete sighed in relief when Kate, after being discharged, stopped drinking. Thinking of the scare she had put in him, he shuddered to think how close to death she had come.

"I don't need a medical report to verify what I know to be true," he thought.

"Another few hours and we would have lost her."

CHAPTER FIVE
A BIRTHDAY; MADDIE TURNS 49

March 2019

It had become Pete's lot to worry about the wreckage that had been left behind. This was a burden made heavier, he knew, by the regret he carried for dragging Mary Lou and the children to Massachusetts and into a life they had not envisioned—and were reluctant to accept. His rashness had triggered much of a negative consequence that had transpired since; that was still happening.

Massachusetts was busier, louder and less agreeable than the environment the family was used to back in New York State. Years after The Move, in fact, Pete came across the results of a study that had determined the Commonwealth to be one of the nation's "most unfriendly" locales. This he attributed to the crusty dispositions, bordering on standoffishness, of New Englanders: the outwardly unwelcoming Yankee persona of a Maine paper-mill or shipyard worker, or a Boston cab driver.

At the same time, it was in his nature to be appreciative of the blessings. He had never been one to complain about problems. He always believed in looking forward. Mary Lou was mystified by where her husband's positivity came from.

"You're the optimist, I'm the pessimist," she would say.

Returning that night to Worcester without the job that had lured him to Massachusetts two and a half years earlier, he could anticipate Mary Lou's reaction. Despite this, he was certain that his prospects would take a turn for the better.

They always had.

II

Maddie was blowing out the candles on her forty-ninth birthday cake on the wind-tossed next-to-last Saturday of the month at her parents' home in Northbridge. This was the duplex they had settled into, in the Blackstone Valley, in 1988, making them residents of "The Birthplace of the American Industrial Revolution." Nearby mills, named for where they were situated—Riverdale, Linwood, Manchaug, Fisherville—had remained in abundance as still-functioning manufacturing plants or as housing.

Pete was capturing the moment with the camera on his cell phone. In a few seconds he would give Maddie the card he and Mary Lou had signed and then watch as she pulled from the gift bag sitting in front of her a plaque he had purchased at a little store in downtown Uxbridge earlier in the week. He had been perusing the store's merchandise—stuffed animals, personalized coffee cups, soaps, handbags, scarves, jewelry, Patriots and Red Sox memorabilia—in search of something she would like. His eyes had settled on the plaque, the frame of which was made of driftwood. There was space in the plaque, which was beach-themed, for a single 4x6 photograph.

"Perfect," he said. "The beach is her favorite place to be."

He had gone through a number of pictures, printed out four of them at CVS and inserted one he especially liked. Maddie was walking towards them at Wells Beach, sand beneath her feet, the ocean to her back. She was taking *Salty Steps*, which was the message conveyed in the lettering on the plaque.

"She will love this!" he thought.

Pete wondered where Maddie would place the plaque. In her perpetual quest to improve the appearance of her home, on a rural road just outside Oxford Center, she had demonstrated a decorator's flair for where photographs and wall mountings should go to achieve maximum impact. She didn't overdo it. She kept these flourishes to a select few, just as she limited the number of furnishings and accessories she had on the floor. She often referred to herself as "a minimalist." She avoided oversaturation and clutter as if they were toxic. Pete wasn't sure where this knack in his daughter came from, but he admired it. He knew others did too. The word "lovely" came to be used more and more in commendation of her skill in making the house on Dudley Road a place that exuded character and charm.

It did not occur to Pete until years after Claude and Maddie had gone from being renters in Worcester to homeowners in Oxford that his daughter's infatuation with creating a residence she could be proud of must have stemmed from her memories of the house on Hoffman Avenue in Vestal. He had his own fond recollections of the place, the newest on the street, into which Horace Nash had poured such labor and perspiration. The children had witnessed the house take shape board by board from the foundation up...how could their thoughts of their grandfather's work not be among the most vivid—and precious—in their possession?

Surely too, Pete realized, they must still be bothered by whatever had motivated him to so casually dismiss the handsome structure Horace Nash had erected for his eldest son, his daughter-in-law, and their children. Hoffman Avenue was a gift far more meaningful than the one Pete and Mary Lou were presenting to Maddie on this particular occasion.

How disappointed Horace Nash must have been to see Hoffman Avenue put up for sale less than ten years after he had nailed the last shingle in place!

Pete's reasoning in leaving Hoffman Avenue behind had never been satisfactorily explained to them.

Small wonder that he had much to answer for, in their minds.

III

With the strains of "Happy Birthday" filling the dining room and Maddie's face aglow from the candles that adorned the vanilla cake that sat in the middle of the dining-room table, Pete whispered a private prayer of thanksgiving.

His family had suffered and would suffer more. More even than Pete and Mary Lou's closest relatives knew the full extent of.

There was, however, cause for celebration.

Madeleine Anne was turning forty-nine. The five of them had managed to get this far.

Whatever grief the future brought, they would deal with it.

Right?

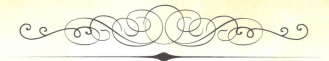

CHAPTER SIX
PETE'S QUANDARY, AND A MOMENTOUS DECISION

April 1986

Nearly a year had passed since Pete went to work in Brookline. Some semblance of order, some degree of routine, had been established among the five of them—but with an uneasiness always lurking. There hung in the air a sense of foreboding.

Pete felt it. They all did.

In the morning they were out the door early, Pete to his job at Citizen Inc. on Harvard St. in Brookline—only a few blocks from Coolidge Corner, where the lithe runners competing in the Boston Marathon came through on weary legs—Mary Lou to the rest home on the north side of Worcester, Maddie to North High on Harrington Way, DJ and Kate to Worcester East Middle on Grafton St.

They had made a grudging peace with the city of Worcester. It wasn't Vestal but it was home, now.

Nothing had been quite the same in the aftermath of Maddie's disappearance. Pete considered the episode to be a closed book. He had handled it. Once the initial shock had worn off, once it had become clear that she wasn't in the immediate vicinity, he had called the Worcester Police Department from the wall telephone in the kitchen on Cohasset St.

"Probably at a friend's house, that's usually how these things go. Have you checked around?" a desk sergeant said in a thick Irish brogue.

Pete would come to love Worcester's St. Patrick's Day Parade, the sight of political people he knew through his role as a newspaperman—who went by the name Murray, Monfredo, Toomey, O'Brien, Mahoney, Rosen, O'Day, Chandler, Economou, O'Sullivan, Evangelista, Binienda, Lukes, Petty, Plant and McGovern—marching down Park

Ave. from Webster Square to Elm Park and waving to spectators. They were a reflection of the diversity that had made the city such a melting pot. He would get into the habit of attending the parade every spring with one or more of his children and grandkids and staking out a spot about midway along the route for a view of the proceedings, those always reinvigorated him. The marching bands. The lavishly decorated floats. The blaring fire trucks. The high-stepping dancers. The candy throwers. The vendors hawking beads and balloons and hats. The tailgaters crammed into the parking lots of bars or of businesses owned by friends of theirs, swigging from red solo cups.

A crowd of 30,000 or so was not unusual. It was a big deal.

At this moment, however, the trace of emerald green hills and valleys and plains on the desk sergeant's tongue only infuriated him.

"We're new to town, she hardly knows anyone," Pete said, his voice cracking.

She hadn't been at school. She wasn't at Julia Cruz's house. She was gone.

"She has to be missing for at least forty-eight hours before we can get involved," the desk sergeant said. "I'm sure she'll show up. Keep trying to locate her. Tell you what. I'll make some inquiries."

Returning the receiver to its cradle, Pete turned. Mary Lou was standing inches away from him, her face already indicating that she knew he had gotten nowhere with the call.

"We'll hear from her," he said, trying to sound hopeful.

His stomach, doing flips, told him maybe they wouldn't.

II

On the evening of the second day Al Jenkins called from Vestal to report that Maddie was "with us. She's okay."

Hearing this, Pete's first reaction was relief, followed by awe and surprise. "The audacity!" he thought. But when his father-in-law told him Maddie had taken a bus to Binghamton and been picked up on Chenango Street by her boyfriend, he could feel the blood rising in his cheeks.

"Your dad says she has no intention of returning," Pete said. "I'm going for her in the morning. She's coming back!"

In his anger Pete did not consider that an uglier development than the one confronting them might have materialized; that Maddie might have been abducted before reaching the small bus terminal on Madison St.; that instead of successfully transferring to a different coach in Albany (how did she manage *that*?) she might have mistakenly boarded one bound for New York City and been collared at the Port Authority by a hustler in a black leather jacket and pimped out. That she might have disappeared without a trace: vanished. "My God!" Pete thought. "Fifteen years old!"

Pete was so incensed by Maddie's disloyalty that he didn't consider until long afterwards how lucky she had been to pull it off.

Lucky; and resourceful.

It never occurred to him to let her remain with Al and Grace Jenkins. It wasn't that they weren't good in-laws or that they didn't mean well. They were in fact the salt of the earth. He understood too why Maddie would have gravitated to Kimble Road as a sanctuary. Their home was within walking distance of the high school. She could have at least finished her sophomore year there. She had slept in an upstairs bedroom, on overnights. She had spent countless Sundays and holidays with her cousins in the company of "Pa" and "Gram" Jenkins.

"But," he reasoned, "to DJ and Kate this would have smacked of favoritism."

Pete's objection to Maddie's intentions was rooted, as his choice of Brookline over Binghamton had been, in part by a need to get away from circumstances—and places—that made him feel as if he was hemmed in. Pa and Grace's home was one of these, as was the newspaper office on the Parkway.

No one, not even Mary Lou, and certainly not the children, knew the depth of his disenchantment.

Mary Lou must have had an inkling, however. How could she not? He had been dropping hints. Surely she could not have missed the clues he was sending.

Something had to change.

III

On their after-dinner walks through the neighborhood Pete had confided to Mary Lou that he and the newspaper's managing editor were at an impasse. They were clashing over the pettiest things.

Pete had known the ME—Lloyd Anderson—since the start of their newspapering days on Henry Street in Binghamton, before the morning tabloid they worked for was gobbled up by the evening broadsheet. Pete was a rookie sportswriter in a three-man department then, lacking in the precociousness that he knew was essential to asking the hard questions, getting the right answers and breaking the big story. Eventually his interviewing technique would improve, based on his ability to put people at ease and entice them to open up.

Lloyd Anderson was a City Hall reporter with a huge ego.

Now they were operating within shouting distance of each other, Pete as news editor in charge of the Universal Desk, Anderson as overseer of all editorial functions from his office: the same space Pete's brother-in-law Lucas Olsen had occupied, before he and Sally Rae relocated to Texas. Anderson, sporting a waistline commensurate with his newfound stature as a rising star in the Gannett Co. galaxy, had taken to second guessing Pete's every decision. At the afternoon Page One meetings at which Pete, Anderson, the local editor, the sports editor, the features editor, the business editor and the food editor gathered to outline their game plan for the next morning's edition, Anderson would challenge Pete's selection of stories to lead with. He would question headlines Pete or his copy editors had written. He would dictate which inside stories should be teased on Page One. With the sleeves of his starched white Fowler's Department Store shirt rolled up and his tie loosened at the neck, Anderson was a constant thorn.

"I can't stomach the guy," Pete told Mary Lou. "He's insufferable. I can remember when he and his pal Chet Colburn spent most of their time at the bar at the Little Venice on Chenango St., tipping them back as Gus O'Leary set them up, instead of checking the police log like they were supposed to."

Early in their marriage Mary Lou had realized that the restless energy Pete was born with would govern the path his career took, just as it would how he spent his nonworking hours. He was helpless to control this drive. Nor did he want to. Two years after exchanging vows at the front of the Methodist church in Vestal they were off to Plattsburgh in the North Country. Pete had taken a job as sports editor of the *Press-Republican*. They stayed only long enough for Mary Lou to give birth to Maddie. A year after that it was on to Newburgh, downstate, where Pete became assistant sports editor of the *Evening News*.

To Mary Lou, he seemed never to be content; always to be searching for something more.

For a while such hobbies as gardening and woodworking and growing tomatoes filled voids. He built a candle box and a table with a top that swung open for Mary Lou. Mary Lou canned the tomatoes he harvested.

Inevitably, he would again be pushed to the brink. He saw persistent interference in his work coming from Lloyd Anderson as a bad omen, Just as he saw the usurping of time he could be spending with his side of the family coming from "mom Jenkins"—Grace—as an unbearable imposition.

He would attach no more importance to one than the other. They were equally responsible for his angst. He could make Mary Lou understand why Lloyd Anderson was a monkey on his back. But Grace? That was more problematic. He hated that it put him and Mary Lou at odds.

IV

As the baby of the Jenkins family, the youngest of Albert and Grace's four children, Mary Lou reveled in the opportunity she had been given to return to the nest. Back in Vestal in 1973, she thought for good—no more roaming to satisfy Pete's wanderlust—she looked forward to spending Sundays with her parents; sitting with Grace for the morning service in the same pew on the right side of the sanctuary that her mother had occupied for many years and then dinner on Kimble Road with her sisters, brother, sister-in-law, brothers-in-law and nieces and nephews surrounding her.

Pete's issue with this arrangement did not stem from any personal animosity toward Albert and Grace or his new relatives by marriage. He was glad for their kinship. Especially that of Lucas and Sally Rae, who had orchestrated the blind date that brought Pete and Mary Lou together over drinks at a tavern on the North Side of Endicott on Christmas Night in 1967. There was an immediate sexual attraction between Pete and Mary Lou but even more than that a compatibility that both recognized as conducive to long-term. Pete loved Mary Lou's striking black hair, rich and full, her vocation (she was an LPN) and what he instantly saw as the sound logic of a mathematician or a jurist. The sterling character, too, of a saint. She was, in his estimation, a woman of substance: well-mannered and down-to-earth. He figured she detected in him a passion for flights of whimsy that might prove interesting—if not always rewarding.

Theirs was a whirlwind romance consummated, literally, in the front and back seats of Mary Lou's pale-yellow VW convertible, to the sounds of The Platters and Nat King Cole and Andy Williams and Carole King on the radio. It was marked by Pete's introduction to their calendar of sporting events that Mary Lou had previously treated mostly with indifference and in Mary Lou's suggestion that they participate in alcohol-enlivened parlor games including Charades at Lucas and Sally Rae's apartment on Jensen Road.

The tradeoff for Pete was buying into Grace Jenkins's regimen, which consisted of church, dinner and a willingness to come around whenever an invitation was extended.

Pete balked. Not because of any disdain for Grace or the things she held important but rather because he found her promotion of them to be overbearing.

V

The church was Grace's Rock of Gibraltar. It was her foundation when Pa drank, before he quit "cold turkey when I was young," as Mary Lou put it; swore off liquor, replacing it with coffee—straight black and keep the cups coming. The church salved Grace's wounds when Albert's occasional irritableness flared, when he smoked in the house or in the car, when he spoke disparagingly of Methodists and Jesus Christ, when he "got loud" with his friend and fellow tinkerer Harold Peters—the two of them talking back and forth at a high decibel level even at close range as their wives, Grace and Peg, shook their heads in disapproval.

She taught Sunday school, a golden agers group of women. She played in the bell choir. She read her Bible, her *Upper Room*, *Guideposts*, devotional literature. She prayed. She wore purple which was her deeply religious hue of choice, and not just at Eastertime. She quoted Scripture.

Having grown up Baptist, a grandson of the maternal Blanche who was, like Grace, a pillar, Pete accepted the premise of worship on Sunday. He exalted Grace for her standing as a decorated Christian soldier. He liked that Maddie, DJ and Kate thought of her as a bastion of decency, good tidings, love for them without any strings attached and champion of the Ten Commandments.

Her insistence on laying claim to his Sundays and holidays at the expense of time with his own parents and brothers, across the river in Owego, was what rankled. As the hours spent with Grace increased, as Pete's attempts to pry Mary Lou loose from her mother's grip failed, his exasperation flared. With each assumption on Grace's part that they would be staying for dinner, going apple picking or rummaging for treasure ("there are yard sales all over town this weekend"), with a realization that time in Owego would be forfeited, Pete could feel the back of his neck turn red. The ensuing friction between Pete and Mary Lou, though unspoken in Grace's presence, was hot to the touch.

Pete's children were too young to recognize the frustration he was feeling. Only Mary Lou could sense his displeasure at what he saw as an unfair arrangement. Pete in turn understood that Mary Lou felt an obligation to spend time with her mother.

That his father-in-law in his recliner in the corner of the Jenkins living room, with his cigarettes and pipe rack and ashtray handy at his elbow, seemed unsympathetic to Pete's plight—that Pa did not step up in Pete's defense—made Pete's predicament that much harder to tolerate.

He did not blame Pa, however. His quarrel was with Grace.

Not even Pete and Grace's mutual fondness for walking could alleviate the tension between them.

No such division existed between Pete and Pa Jenkins.

He didn't want it to, either, between he and Grace.

On periodic returns to Vestal, in the years that followed, Grace, now living in a nursing home, greeted Pete warmly. Sitting in her wheelchair in the sun, conversing with Pete and Mary Lou, she and Pete chatted amicably. His affection for his mother-in-law offset any remembrances of prior resentments.

Differences that had existed between them were a thing of the past.

CHAPTER SEVEN

PETE AND PA, COMMON GROUND; MADDIE, RESISTING

Pa Jenkins' aversion to Grace's overarching Methodism was negated in Pete's mind by his father-in-law's affinity for handyman-like initiatives. These could run the gamut. Pete sought to do as Pa did. Never had Pete seen a workbench like Albert maintained in the basement, where beneath the glow of a seemingly ever-burning shop light he repaired broken clocks and broken zippers and broken picture frames and broken tea kettles and broken toys. Pa owned every tool imaginable. Drills and saws and clamps and vices and levels and squares, every nut and bolt and nail and washer all of which were carefully organized in glass jars that Grace had washed and put aside for him. A wood lathe, too, that Pa would eventually pass on to Pete; the carving and shaping tools that went with it, also. These remained in Pete's possession.

More even than a workbench of equal worth Pete wanted Pa's mechanical capabilities. He wanted his reputation as a Mr. Fix-It, his brain that was hardwired for solutions to the thorniest problem involving gadgets: a God-given talent that Mary Lou was endowed with as well; that Pete never would acquire.

Pete thought of himself as the one of Pa's three sons-in-law who was most keen on absorbing the technique that Pa Jenkins could demonstrate to him as mentor. The other side of Pete, from his newspaper work and reading and writing, became an adaptation of his father-in-law. Pete took out a subscription to *Early American Life*, built Mary Lou a mirror with beveled edges, started a compost pile with the shredded leaves and debris from a chipper that Pa let him borrow, used Pa's rototiller to churn the ground for planting, helped Pa reside his house and replace old flooring on the front porch with tongue-and-groove boards, helped him move the steps to the porch from the front to the side, accompanied Pa to Vestal Lumber or Central Tractor for items his father-in-law needed, soaked up Pa's instruction on how to change the oil in Pete and Mary Lou's Chevelle, to avoid wasting paint ("poke a few holes in the rim with a nail so that the paint drips back into the can") and how to install new webbing on a folding aluminum lawn chair.

Pete did not see Albert Jenkins as an adversary.

He wished he didn't see Grace as one either.

VII

Pete had misread the depth of Maddie's despair. Years later, in thinking back on the string of hardships that The Move brought, his mind would always return to the specter of Maddie on the run. Sometimes he had to pinch himself in wondering if all the crises that followed her bold denunciation of his plan were real or just a bad dream. Would all three of the Nash children still have quit school before graduating and had to obtain their GED? Would all of them have taken up smoking? Would he have been able to walk Kate down the aisle, as he had Maddie, instead of watching her reach her mid-forties unmarried? Would DJ never have set foot in a jail cell, a psych ward, a courtroom, a halfway house?

In his heart he knew that these outcomes had indeed materialized. There was no denying it. In asserting his authority, in driving to Vestal, in informing Pa and Grace that Maddie must accompany him back to Worcester, Pete was certain that he had broken her will. Instead he had underestimated her capacity to defy him.

Two weeks after Maddie tested Pete, Pa and Grace arrived on Cohasset St. for a visit. Pete and Mary Lou were accustomed to the Jenkins's checking up on them, just as Horace and Beatrice Nash did. Both sets of parents had ventured to Plattsburgh in 1970 right after Maddie was born, and to Newburgh in 1972 when Pete and Mary Lou, with two-year-old Maddie in tow, were settling into a second-floor apartment just off Broadway.

This was different. Pete was conscious of the curiosity that was prompting the Jenkins's quickly made decision to come east. "It's a pretense, they want to know that there are no negative aftereffects from the stunt Maddie pulled," he thought. "They also want to make sure I am not the ogre I appear to be."

A hush had fallen over the house that Friday evening when Pete climbed the stairs to he and Mary Lou's bedroom. He had stayed up later than usual to satisfy himself that everyone was asleep. Over dinner he had told Maddie that with her grandparents in town she couldn't go to the Outlets Mall with Julia Cruz. He had shrugged off her pout.

Mary Lou had closed the Maeve Binchey book she was reading, put her hearing aids away and turned out the lamp on the nightstand.

Pete crawled into bed.

A commotion roused him. The face of the alarm clock showed 12:35 a.m.

"Maddie's room," he thought. Reaching it, he caught a fleeting glimpse of her as she jumped out the second-floor window. "This can't be happening!" he thought.

Pete raced down the stairs, through the kitchen, into the backyard. He grabbed Maddie by her hair and hauled her inside.

"I hate you!" you screamed.

"Shh," he whispered. "You'll wake your grandparents!"

The next morning, Pa and Grace gave no indication that the disturbance had roused them. For all Pete knew, they had slept through it.

CHAPTER EIGHT
FIRE ON COHASSET ST.

On his daily commute from Grafton Hill by way of the Mass Pike to Brookline, Pete had time to sort out the pros and cons of life in Massachusetts; to consider whether accepting the editorship of The Citizen's three weekly tabloids amounted to a plus or a minus. Whether, also, the choice of Worcester as a place of residence was conducive to success for the family—or a recipe for failure.

Increasingly, he was plagued by misgivings.

These he would mull while listening to the radio, tuned to WBZ (1030 AM), a twenty four-hour news channel with traffic, weather and sports. He had taken a liking to the voices of Gary LaPierre and Jon Keller. WBZ's 50,000 watts also negated any chance of static, which he couldn't tolerate.

To Pete the forty miles of the Turnpike he covered each morning, clogged as the highway was, herd of cattle-like, especially around the Weston toll booths, would have been impossible to tolerate without LaPierre's description of happenings that were garnering notice in the Commonwealth. Pete's spirits were invariably lifted by the steady drumbeat of information provided to him by the talking heads on his favorite channel on the dial, just as many years later he would be soothed by WUMB (91.9 FM) out of UMass Boston, which offered hour after hour of music featuring artists he had come to admire.

On the road after he had discovered WUMB, Pete would be captivated by the sounds of Chris Smither, Tom Waits, Richard Thompson, Emmylou Harris, John Hiatt, Lucinda Williams, John Prine, Mavis Staples, Mary Gauthier, Roseann Cash, Levon Helm, The Avett Brothers and Rodney Crowell.

"How could I not have stumbled across these people years ago?" he would ask himself. They satisfied his yearning for lyrics that could not be construed as "pop crap."

Pete appreciated that he was bound to thousand of fellow wayfaring strangers en route to jobs in the city from Brockton, Newton, Somerville, Framingham, Natick and Westborough—from Central Massachusetts, the North Shore and the South Shore—by this dependence on WBZ. He liked knowing that they, like him, part of a swarm of humanity, were invested in what they were hearing. Everything, in Pete's mind, rode, literally, on the exuberance of Gary LaPierre's reporting and Jon Keller's astute political analysis.

Keller often gave him something more to ponder in his time slot at five minutes before eight o'clock and that was a diatribe against bad driving. "So true, so true," Pete would say, in affirmation of Keller lecturing his listeners on the importance of keeping two hands on the wheel, on avoiding the urge to change lanes, on staying focused and not being distracted, on refraining from tailgating and on observing posted speed limits.

It was as if LaPierre and Keller were telling him he mattered.

"I am a Bay Stater and a Bostonian," Pete would think, in convincing himself that he was entitled to all of the rights and privileges that came with being an adopted son of the Commonwealth; suppressing, as he did so, the notion that Mary Lou, Maddie, DJ and Kate might not share his zeal for what the birthplace of American freedom should mean to them—in terms of an identity with an historically significant part of the country.

In his euphoria Pete refused to acknowledge that the difficulties The Move had created for Mary Lou and the children had left them less than ecstatic. Driving in each morning, he was blinded by the sun rising over the Atlantic, bathing South Station, Quincy Market, Charlestown, the North End, Logan Airport, the State House, Boston Common and the Financial District in shimmering light. At the same time, his perception of Boston needing him, meriting his presence—and his family's loyalty—was clouded by an awareness of experiences he had enjoyed while Mary Lou was trying to sell the property in Vestal and manage the kids. While she was running a household he was shaking hands with Holocaust survivor Elie Wiesel at Boston University, watching the Red Sox from a seat in the bleachers and reveling in the gold-embossed invites he had received to the grand opening of the Embassy Suites and Four Seasons hotels and to the maiden voyage of the *Spirit of Boston*.

He did not once stop and ask himself "why am I being so selfish?"

II

Pete had discovered as a boy that there is often the odor of smoke before there is the sight of flame, just as there is the scent of a skunk before its carcass is seen on the road. Still, despite what he knew about the house on Cohasset St.—that it was ninety years old and in much sorrier shape than other homes on Grafton Hill—he was unprepared for the acrid smell that reached his nostrils as he and Mary Lou ate breakfast, that morning.

A year and a half into their new life in Worcester, it was already apparent to them that the city had not been kind to the children. Maddie had dropped out of North High and was on the verge of being banished from the house by Mary Lou, in a mother-daughter spat. Maddie's efforts to flee Massachusetts having been thwarted, she would make no further tries. Instead she would somehow find her way on her own, settling into a job cashiering at a Honey Farms on Park Ave. and securing a tiny apartment on the west side of the city, near Elm Park. A small network of friends would become her anchor.

In retrospect Pete realized he should have given Maddie the credit she deserved for demonstrating the will to carry on, so soon after he had reined her in. Much later he would marvel at the first stirrings of fight in the bosom of a girl who until then had been bashful and compliant. These, expressed, initially, in her desperate bid to get away, and then in absences from school that would lead to her refusal to show up for class at all.

"Where are you going?" Pete asked one morning when, acting on a hunch, he altered his route to work by taking Hamilton St. instead of Grafton St. out to the Pike. He found Maddie and Julia Cruz walking not towards Harrington Way but in the direction of Julia's house. "Get in," he said. "You'll be late for first bell."

Pete was in no hurry to praise Maddie for the ingenuity she had shown in attempting to extract herself from a situation she deplored.

By this time too DJ and Kate had moved from Dartmouth Street to Worcester East Middle, which, as the Nash family fate would have it, amounted to sacrificial lambs being sent to slaughter. The imposing, fortress-like structure was austere to look at from the outside and then there would be neighborhood hoodlums to contend with. Soon after beginning seventh grade, DJ was in constant fear for his safety.

Had Pete been possessed of better judgment, he might even then have said "this isn't working" and taken the family back to Vestal—somehow. He might have realized that the adjustment he was asking of Mary Lou and the children was not only unachievable but an omen of darker days ahead.

In his typical stubborn fashion, he assured himself that all was well.

Or at least salvageable.

III

Scrambling up the stairs, Pete at the door to he and Mary Lou's bedroom saw the long beige curtains engulfed. Flames were licking the walls and snaking toward the ceiling.

There was no time to consider DJ's daily struggle to mesh with a culture that seethed with animus toward him. No time to think about talks Pete and Mary Lou had been having with DJ's guidance counselors.

"Get out! Everyone out!" Pete screamed.

The scene that unfolded over the next several minutes was surreal. Neighbors they hadn't yet met materializing as if by hocus pocus to join them in the middle of Farrar Ave. or gawking at the sudden catastrophe from their yards. People, dogs, cats and now fire trucks and firefighters in a made-for-the-six-o'clock-news moment, thick fire hoses spread across the street, a ladder extended to the roof, two men clad in fire-retardant yellow jackets and helmets hacking at the shingles with axes, water pouring into the gaping hole they made.

Pete was so caught up in the preposterousness of this latest crushing blow that he didn't see a photographer off to the side, snapping pictures, one of which would run with a short story on the front of the B section of that afternoon's newspaper.

His mind was a jumble of questions.

"Can they save our house?"

"What is Fred going to say when I tell him I can't make it to work today? He is already on my back for not being invested enough in Citizen Inc.

"Can Mary Lou and the children ever forgive me for thinking only of me and my career?

"Why are Worcester, and Massachusetts, so inhospitable to us?"

IV

The state fire marshal delivered his ruling about the cause of the blaze—faulty wiring—about a week later. Pete and Mary Lou were left to contemplate the significance of the declaration; obviously, Pete thought, inadequate electrical service, installed who knows when, was tangible proof of his wrongheadedness in requiring Mary Lou and the children to buy into his foolish notion that moving to Massachusetts would be no more problematic that slipping into a pair of jeans.

He could not help but see the charred remains of the second floor and the extensive water damage to the first floor as misfortune having tagged him for the suffering he was due. The portrait of their life in all its ugliness was coming together: his motorcycle accident, the tenuousness of his circumstances trying to understand Fred Phelps's muddled strategy for his weekly newspapers, the seven months it had taken Mary Lou to close the deal in Vestal, last-minute word from the attorney representing the couple selling the Worcester property that the closing date would have to be delayed (hearing this, Mary Lou, staying with she and Pete's friends Dick and Gretchen Boardman near Albany, replied "the closing date stands or I'm going back to Vestal—I don't need this!"), Maddie's brief but unnerving disappearance, the beginning of DJ and Kate's reliance on alcohol to cope with their insecurities and now the fire.

The five of them would spend the next three months living in the Days Inn on Lincoln St. while the cleanup and the rebuild of the upstairs progressed. Pete in his mortification over the family's run of bad luck would drive by Cohasset St. to see the dumpster in the front yard filled with debris that was being tossed out the window of the master bedroom, including prized possessions, and wonder "what next?"

Fred Phelps pretended to be sympathetic and understanding but Pete could sense his boss's impatience with an editor he had handpicked to lead Citizen Inc. from obscurity to widespread acceptance.

Parishioners at the Methodist church on Hamilton St. that the Nash's had been attending took up a collection. Pastor Mike presented Pete and Mary Lou with an envelope. Inside was nine hundred dollars.

"See," Pete said to Mary Lou. "New Englanders aren't the cold people they're known as.

"Life is good."

CHAPTER NINE

'I CAN'T BELIEVE WE'RE NOT ALL DEAD'

A strange phenomenon, Pete and Mary Lou, products of what so many in Broome County in the 1950s referred to as "Eisenhower country," Republican-leaning (in contrast to the "Blue"-voting stronghold of NYC, and much of downstate), Protestant-leaning, now surrounded on all sides in Massachusetts by Democrats and Catholics.

It was another outcome of The Move that Pete had not prepared himself for. These were adding up. He, they, were the victims of his own shortsightedness in not seeing far enough ahead to know that Central Massachusetts was not upstate New York. He wasn't aware of one three decker in Vestal, only small ranches and Capes. Worcester was famous for them.

Pete was the eldest of Horace and Beatrice's four sons, Mary Lou the youngest of Albert and Grace's one son and three daughters. Theirs, in Endicott and Vestal, on opposite sides of the Susquehanna River, had been a sheltered existence. As the firstborn, Pete had reaped the benefits of being the first in line for the fawning attention provided to him by his parents, grandparents, aunts and uncles. As the last to come along, Mary Lou was accorded the courtesies generally reserved for the one in the family who is viewed as the most breakable. Pete would be seen as the senior statesman by his brothers and Mary Lou as the child-we-need-to-treat-with-TLC by her brother and sisters for all of their lives.

They were baptized not only in the religion of their parents but in a certainty that their lives would follow an established pattern. Mary Lou's choice of nursing and Pete's of journalism for their careers echoed that of their forbears in opting to work on the farm, in construction, in the factory. There was also an assumption that they would not stray many miles from the community in which their youth had been spent. They would remain part of a familial network that was deeply rooted in the soil of Broome County. There would be no need to venture out from a place that had produced a celebrated horror and science fiction writer (Rod Serling), a major league shortstop (Johnny Logan of the

Milwaukee Braves), an aeronautics pioneer (Edwin Link) and a Jim Thorpe-like athlete (Vestal's own Bobby Campbell, who would star at Penn State). The tendency of twenty somethings to look beyond the parameters of "The Valley of Opportunity" that had fed them, clothed them, educated them and shielded them was not yet the craze it would become in the later years of the 20th Century.

Mary Lou would have been content to remain in Vestal; to stay within arm's reach of her mother and father.

Pete had other ideas.

He could justify these by telling himself that he wouldn't be the first to pull up stakes. Mary Lou's brother Bruce and his wife Alice had left for South Carolina and would eventually wind up in Ohio. Her sister Sally Rae and brother-in-law Lucas for Texas and then Iowa, Delaware, Maine and finally Rochester, New York. Younger members of the family would follow suit.

There was this, too: when Pete told Pa Jenkins that he was being offered a better salary and a better job in Brookline his father-in-law had replied "a man's got to make a decent living."

Pa was not known for wordiness. He was known for irrefutable logic. His words mattered.

Hearing Pa's answer, Pete thought, "what other endorsement do I need than the blessing of a wise old owl of a father-in-law who, when I first joined the Jenkins family for Sunday dinner, said to Mary Lou, as he had to Sarah and Sally Rae, "if you can sleep with him, I can eat with him.""

II

With the conclusion of the six o'clock service at the Methodist church on Hamilton Street on Christmas Eve, they shook hands with Pastor Mike and walked out of the building into a cold and dark night. Pete did not think much of the moisture with which the air was laden as the five of them started toward the Le Baron, which was parked along the curb halfway up the hill.

The dampness, however, carried a portent of ill tidings.

He was much more conscious of the tenuous hold he had on his job at Citizen Inc. Fred Phelps' impulsive moves as publisher were exacerbated only by a refusal to accept results that left him uninspired, Pete often recalled the interview that had brought him to Brookline in the spring of 1985, how impressed he was by Fred's infectious enthusiasm as they chatted across the desk that Fred sat behind in his office. Pete read Fred's exuberance in talking up his grand design for his publications and the wining and dining that followed as a signal that the job was ideal for him.

Phelps was a short man whose haircut, combined with a flamboyant persona, marked by a nervous but contagious energy, reminded Pete of Richard Simmons leading workouts on television. What impressed Pete most was Phelps' Boston accent and his promotion of the city as one of the country's most prestigious places to live and work. Pete was sold on the job even before lunch at a fancy restaurant a few blocks away at Coolidge Corner, Phelps wheeling his BMW through the back streets at a frenetic pace and across the tracks of the Green Line and then coming to a halt in a no-parking zone outside the front door.

"A table with a little privacy, hon," he said to the hostess as he burst inside, the hands in his cuff-linked shirt grabbing for a menu.

In retrospect it occurred to Pete that there would have been no need for Fred Phelps to take the circuitous route to the restaurant, as a cabbie would in running up the meter on a fare. He would never have had to leave Harvard Street. It was a matter of Fred showboating for his prospective new editor. It was also Fred dealing with private doubts that must have gnawed at him about his capacity to compete for advertising dollars and reader patronage in a media market dominated by the two large dailies and by the *Boston Phoenix.*

Fred Phelps enjoyed wowing people this way. Two weeks later Mary Lou and the children came to Boston for a dinner that Fred and Judith treated them to at the Howard Johnson's on the Mass Pike. "Dad!" Maddie, DJ and Kate exclaimed, "this hotel is built right over the highway!" It was true. Scurrying to the windows of the dining room, they could see traffic passing underneath the building.

Like their father, they pictured Fred Phelps as some kind of big shot.

III

Pete and Mary Lou were glad for Route 88, one hundred forty miles of newly constructed road connecting Albany and Binghamton—named for longtime New York Sen. Warren M. Anderson of Dickinson. "What a godsend," they thought. Still fresh in their memory were the eight hours it had taken them, on Route 7 and other two-lane roads through the North Country, to get to Plattsburgh when Pete worked there, or the four and a half it took them to reach the state capital going back and forth between Vestal and Worcester, before Route 88 was built.

They could overlook the tediousness of the ride on a largely desolate ribbon of highway with nothing much to look at except the exit signs for Howe Caverns and Cobleskill and Cooperstown and Oneonta in appreciation of being able to maintain a speed of seventy miles per hour and reaching their destination in about five hours' time.

To give his eyes a break, Pete had turned the wheel over to Mary Lou for the last portion of the trip. Maddie, DJ and Kate were half asleep in the back seat as the five of them made the dash for home and Christmas morning at Pa and Grace's place. They would arrive before midnight.

Pete was fiddling with the radio, flipping the knob in an effort to find music in an area where reception was poor. Static drove him crazy. He would do anything, listen to most anything, to avoid it.

They had reached the top of an incline about one mile before the rest stop just east of Oneonta when a light snow that had been falling turned to sleet.

They were starting the descent when the Le Baron began to fishtail. Pete glanced at the speedometer. Mary Lou had eased the pedal to fifty-five miles per hour but even that was too fast on a road surface that suddenly offered no traction.

"Don't step on the brake!" Pete heard himself say.

In his subsequent recollections of that night, Pete would always see the car plunging off the highway and rolling over and over down the embankment. Ambulances racing to the scene. Traffic reduced to a snarl. Instead, despite

Mary Lou's firm grip and unflustered concentration, the car swerved from side to side for what seemed like an eternity and then ricocheted off the guardrail and came to a stop in the median.

Pete waited for his heartbeat to slow. He took a breath. He looked out the passenger's-side window and watched as one car after another lost bite and spun. He saw a large tractor trailer somehow maintain both its speed and its course and roar past them, granules of precipitation kicking up in its wake.

"Are you okay?" he asked.

Mary Lou's white-knuckled hands were still on the steering wheel, in the proper position. She had done nothing wrong. He turned. Maddie and DJ were coiled together. Kate was coiled in a ball on the floor.

"I can't believe we're not all dead," he said.

CHAPTER TEN

PETE AND DJ: AN ALTERCATION

DJ"s love for his father, and Pete's for him, carried them through the years. At any number of junctures, because of the havoc caused by DJ's drinking—and Pete's confusion about how to deal with it—it might not have been enough.

Theirs was a bond cemented by Pete's conviction that DJ, unlike many alcoholics, was sincere in his resolve to cure himself. The problem was, he had lost so much—his marriage, his home, to some extent his relationship with his three daughters, his driver's license, jobs, friends—that it seemed as if he would never be able to recoup.

Still he tried. Still he stayed faithful to AA's 12 Steps, hugging his newfound sobriety as he might have a life raft. Still he preached the empowering impact of abstinence. Still he devoured passages from the Bible. Still he prayed for salvation and for good outcomes for loved ones: his mother, his nieces and nephew, his daughters and grandchildren when they came along. Still he wrote poems to anyone and everyone, pouring out his soul in rhyme. Horace Nash had done so before him. This was the impetus DJ needed to follow his grandfather's lead.

Pete saw DJ not as the failure or the pariah he had become in his own mind, and in those of others—including his closest family members—but as the son whose desire to do right, emanating from deep within him, was worth defending. This was what made it so hard: when he fell short of Pete's expectations, when his reliance on his father for support seemed to be too much of an imposition, Pete would feel sorry for himself and swear he would pull away—as Mary Lou had.

"I can't do it," she told Pete. "I love him but my heart needs a rest."

Pete could not do the same. He had vowed to own the guilt he felt for having initiated all of the troubles that accompanied The Move. Also, he could not help but contrast his boyhood in Endicott, which had been so rewarding in every possible way—with DJ's in Worcester; and after that in Northbridge.

He had to make amends, for however long it would take.

II

By September of 2018 and Pete and Mary Lou's 50th wedding anniversary, DJ's difficulties appeared to Pete to be piled as high as the cone-shaped sand dunes he'd seen from a distance while driving the lower end of the Cape, toward Provincetown, in days gone by. DJ had been sober for some time but now there was his dependence on a smorgasbord of medications including Suboxone—dispensed weekly at a clinic in Worcester—to get by and so, Pete told himself, he was still hooked; just on a different substance than alcohol. Also, he hadn't been able to shake the edginess that surfaced whenever he felt he was being maligned. This had caused many a strained moment between them.

One of those that Pete would never forget occurred when they were leaving Maddie's place a few nights before Thanksgiving in 2013, after a birthday party for DJ's Alise. Snow had begun to fall in Oxford. Pete was hating the idea of the drive over treacherous, twisting roads to Douglas, where DJ was living with an acquaintance from AA who had taken him in after DJ's mother-in-law, who had done the same, threw him out.

Theirs—DJ's and Margaret Miller's—was a strained relationship. As for Pete, he didn't know what to make of Margaret.

For starters, she seemed to have not much tolerance for men. Probably, Pete speculated, because Kylie's father had ditched the family long before DJ met and married her. Old man Miller had apparently not been heard from since. Kyle appeared not to have ever known him.

There was also Margaret's multiple sclerosis to consider. She made it clear soon after Pete and Mary Lou met her that she was ill, that MS might be the death of her, that maybe she was due a little consideration on that account.

Pete could make no sense of her living arrangements, either. In addition to her live-in girlfriend, Lila (they would eventually marry), Margaret took in boarders. Any number of people including a furtive and secretive character named Samuel, who had quarters in the basement, resided under her roof. Pete saw the hangers-on, and the vehicles parked in the yard (some of which were rusting in place) as evidence that Margaret Miller was a woman who preferred to exist in a state of constant upheaval.

The general consensus too was that Margaret was "working the system." That she understood the ins and outs of qualifying for assistance. That this was how she footed the bill for electricity, food, heat. Whether this was true or not, the rumor floated in the air like smoke from the chimney at the Wheelabrator trash-disposal facility in Millbury that Pete could see from miles away.

Early in DJ and Kyle's marriage, Margaret challenged them in court for custody of their first-born, Alexandra. The protracted battle—Margaret contending that they weren't suitable parents, DJ and Kylie fighting back—turned DJ against his mother-in-law. DJ and Kylie eventually prevailed, but DJ would never let go of the resentment he felt for Margaret "meddling in our business."

It was one of the few instances during their time together that DJ and Kyle were on the same page.

Against this background Pete and Mary Lou accepted Margaret as a fellow grandparent-in-arms. Besides, her distrust of DJ—the same suspicions about what he was up to that would prompt her to inspect his room in the basement for alcohol or drugs when he was not around—did not extend to them. She held Pete and Mary Lou up as "good people." She continually praised them for their love for the grandchildren. They gave her credit for feeling the same way.

As was his nature, Pete took a big picture point of view. He liked that Margaret was willing to take DJ in despite reservations about his willingness to behave as she expected him to.

He viewed Margaret, a small woman with black hair cut like a boy's, as an equal.

Pete and Margaret got along fine.

III

The prospect of crawling up the steep hill to Tate Lincoln's house had darkened Pete's mood.

He was worrying too about how to tell DJ about a decision he had made.

They were waiting for the traffic light in the center of Oxford to change with snowflakes spattering across the windshield when Pete said "I need to cut back on Sunday visits with your girls now that we're going to church again and Amory's been doing that with us. So we'll have coffee and donuts with the church folks after the service, the three of us, maybe go back to your place for an hour and then I have to be on my way home so mom isn't alone for too long. You know she doesn't like that I leave her for all the running around I do."

He knew that even saying this gently was no guarantee that DJ would take it well.

Out of the corner of his eye Pete saw DJ stiffen. The light turned green. Pete drove on, dreading the nerve-wracking ride he faced and the sullenness his announcement had provoked in DJ.

As Pete inched his way toward the turnoff for the shortcut that would take them past the silos of Whittier Farms in Sutton and on into Douglas he was aware of DJ seething next to him. DJ did not say a word the whole ride. There was only forty minutes of excruciating silence. Pete's stomach was doing somersaults as he tried to concentrate on the road. He was conscious of all the times DJ's anger had boiled over.

Pete shifted the car into a lower gear on the climb to Tate Lincoln's place and held his breath as the tires grabbed. In the driveway DJ opened the door, got out and with his hands balled in fists and large flakes falling onto the shoulders of his black woolen coat said "come on, right now! I always say there are three things you don't mess with, a man's faith, his family and his food!"

"How ridiculous is this?" Pete thought.

He reached across, pulled the passenger-side door shut and backed away.

As he turned his head for a last look before continuing on, Pete saw DJ standing ankle-deep in snow.

Pete was overcome by the emotion of the moment.

"How I love him," he thought.

IV

"We have been through the thick of it, DJ and I," Pete told himself. He thought of Mavis Staples singing about how her mother often said to her "tomorrow will be a better day." As someone who typically looked on the bright side, Pete was sure that the new dawn would bring DJ relief from the woes and worries that constantly besieged him; and that the five of them would finally be able to say "yesterday was just an aberration...we are a family undeterred by the wounds life inflicts. Tomorrow will be better."

Still, in sharing the latest with his brother Roy and sister-in-law Francie, who came to Massachusetts on a surprise visit, bearing gifts and an invitation to dinner out in celebration of Pete and Mary Lou's silver milestone, he could not help but wonder if his positivity wasn't in fact warranted. DJ had marked a forty-fourth birthday in January but was no closer to slipping the shackles that prevented him from finally achieving peace of mind. As DJ's fortunes went, so went Pete's—as confidante, encourager, chauffeur and bank roller.

Pete knew that even in divulging to his brother and sister-in-law (who graciously picked up the tab for dinner at a nearby restaurant) what they were eager to hear of the children—and grandchildren—the account would be incomplete. He was pleased that they cared enough to ask, as he did in inquiring of them how their son Greg and his wife Marilyn and their children were doing since relocating to Charleston, and how Pete's niece Sophie was coping in the aftermath of a shocking end to her marriage.

No secrets were kept between Pete and his brother and sister-in-law.

But no matter how much Pete took them into his confidence, many of the more troubling details were left unrevealed.

All the four of them could be sure of as they continued to talk over coffee was that DJ's ultimate fate—and that of the Nash family—still hung in the balance.

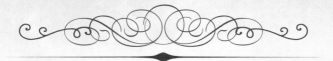

CHAPTER ELEVEN
'I won't puff the cuffs on him, Pete'

How did we get here? Pete asked himself this question over and over. After a while the ups and downs and highs and lows of he and DJ's relationship became almost a blur, like the type in the newspaper that he could no longer read without magnification.

But even then, in trying to recall specifics that eluded him, he was conscious of certain incidents, certain scenes and certain moments that remained fresh in his mind. He thought frequently of times of jubilation and times of sorrow, wondering, as he did so, whether the final tally for the family would amount to a plus or a minus.

"It won't be long before we know," he told himself in the late spring of 2019. "I'm seventy-three, Mary Lou is seventy-one. The picture will come clearly into focus, as it does when Mary Lou adjusts the binoculars to get a sharper look at cardinals nestled in the branches of the burning bush in the backyard. It has to, we don't have forever to know how this is going to turn out for us."

In times of reflection, Pete would try to determine if the good outweighed the bad. There was, foremost in the plus column, he and Mary Lou's union, which had survived Mary Lou even telling him, more than once, when he brought DJ or Kate back into the house over her objections, "I'll move out. You can live with them. You'd be happier without me around."

His assurances to her that this isn't what he wanted seemed to Mary Lou to be insincere. Pete, however, meant it. He just couldn't control the urges in him where the children were concerned. Their difficulties he took on as his own, even while telling himself "this is the last time."

There was too he and Mary Lou's seven grandchildren and three great grandchildren; ten youngsters who provided them with the same life-sustaining lift that a blood transfusion would have. "The flock" was expanded with the birth of Ned to Alexandra and her husband Murphy on St. Patrick's Day 2019. In Cassandra, Jocelyn, Alexandra, Mitchell, Evelyn, Alise, Amory and now Tyler, Beverly (Murphy's by a previous relationship) and Ned the circle was complete.

DJ"s issues nevertheless consumed many of Pete's hours, awake or asleep. Pete thought of them as stretching behind the two of them, like a minefield they had somehow managed to tiptoe through without being mailed or killed.

One of the first involved a run-in DJ had when he was sixteen with "Sgt. Benny" in neighboring Uxbridge. Pete got drawn into the affair, as he so often did in his efforts to keep DJ out of jail.

Benjamin Emerson was a veteran officer with a puffy face and pot belly who had become a prized commodity to "townies" for having patrolled Main Street for years on foot or in a cruiser. He would raise a pudgy hand in cheerful acknowledgement upon hearing the shout of "Benny!" ringing in his ears. He loved using the loudspeaker in his car to bark an order at a pedestrian: "you're jaywalking, mister, use the crosswalk, won't ya;" or, noticing a bunch of kids hanging out in front of the Depot Café, "no loitering, that's a fifty-dollar fine, don't you know?" Pete was vaguely familiar with him as someone whose celebrity had gone to his head.

When DJ told Pete, after being arraigned on a charge of assault in Uxbridge District Court, "I didn't lay a finger on Benny, dad, he caught me and Billy Jacobs drinking, that's all, I swear," Pete wrote a letter to Jack Colton. Pete was counting on the several "puff pieces" he had written on the Uxbridge police chief and his department to make his plea that DJ was being unfairly accused.

Pete dropped the letter in the mailbox and waited.

Chief Colton did not respond.

Subjected to the indignity of having to empty his pockets and remove his belt and shoes as he passed through the metal detector and then having to sit on a hard bench in the courtroom to wait for the call of "all rise," Pete was overcome by self-pity. If he had known then that he would be required to accompany DJ to court over and over—in Uxbridge, in Dudley, in Woburn, in Worcester—he would have thrown up his hands in surrender. If he had known he would have to enlist the services of he and Mary Lou's attorney, Richard Ramstrom of Ramstrom & Ramstrom in Shrewsbury, to represent DJ, at an exorbitant fee, he might have balked. Instead, thinking only of DJ's welfare, he dug into their bank account, just as he had to send DJ to Outward Bound.

"Let me handle this," Ramstrom told DJ, in the courthouse parking lot. Pete was certain that Ramstrom, red-haired, freckle-faced, sartorially dressed and brimming with middle-age swagger, would come through for them.

Still, the tension he felt would not go away.

"You're a little out of your domain, aren't you, counselor?" Judge Arthur Tashjian asked, as he peered over his spectacles in welcoming Ramstrom to Uxbridge District Court.

"I am, your honor, yes sir," Ramstrom replied. "Good to see you, judge."

"He knows all the right moves, all the right words," Pete thought, as he watched Ramstrom stroke the judge as he would a favorite cat.

Judge Tashjian in his black robe had a reputation for leniency. Everyone knew he listened from his perch high above the floor of the courtroom and then gave offenders the benefit of a second chance. Or a third or fourth.

Pete hoped it was true.

As it turned out, DJ never had to take the stand. In cross examining Benny, Ramstrom caught him in a lie.

"You said in the police report that my client kicked you in the shins, is that correct?" Ramstrom asked. He was pacing back and forth in front of the witness box in his blue pinstriped suit and red power tie, smiling at the female stenographer, basking in the stir he had made as a big-city lawyer affording the local yokels a chance to see him operate with the special Ramstrom flair that had been passed on to him by his father.

Benny fidgeted. Benny squirmed.

"Well, he *pushed* me before he and his pal took off."

"Which is it, then, sergeant?" Ramstrom asked.

"What I meant was, he *acted* like he was going to *hit* me," Benny stammered. He shifted in an effort to get comfortable and looked around the courtroom as if in search of someone to corroborate his version of the incident.

"He just *ran*, isn't that right?" Ramstrom asked. "He took off. He didn't actually touch you?"

Benny's face went blank.

There was a long pause.

Pete was surprised by what happened next.

"Sergeant, get your facts straight!" Judge Tashjian said, his dark eyes blazing beneath his black eyebrows.

The judge slammed the file folder down.

"Case dismissed!"

II

There existed within the town of Auburn in the 1980's, not far from the interstate highway and the vast acreage occupied by Polar Beverages, just over the line from Worcester, a deep, wide, concave-shaped "bowl," its walls covered with cement. It was utilized, as DJ related it to Pete long after the fact, as a drainage ditch for spillover from wetlands that often flooded.

It was one of many places to which DJ, under the influence or not, would gravitate, alone or with friends, to test his mettle. It was his way of refuting any notion that he was "chicken;" that alcohol was the only thing he could be defined by. Quarry Hill atop W. Hartford Ave. in Uxbridge where he and his cronies would dive off rocks into a shallow pool of water with little regard for their personal safety was another, as was a rope swing over the road and into "the Res" in Douglas until the Douglas PD took it down. So too the firecrackers that DJ set off while standing near the edge of the bay at Hampton Beach on family vacations for the enjoyment of his nieces and nephew as their parents whispered "don't go near him, he's been drinking." So too his use of a cloth or brush soaked with gasoline to scrub his arms and legs with as a treatment for poison ivy. Pete blanched at the thought of so radical a solution.

DJ had cheated death over and over and not just by the increasingly abundant amount of alcohol he ingested. He wanted to show that he belonged and to some extent that he was living up to his reputation as a "bad boy."

Pete was reading the morning *Telegram* when a five-inch story in the Local section caught his eye. He might have skipped right past it and on into the obituaries and comics except that he knew "briefs" often carried information

54

of more import than major exposes. He therefore never ignored these: world-news shorts, photos accompanied only by a caption, isolated inflammatory quotations that he suspected might mushroom in their provocative nature into World War III.

Pete found something about the story disturbing even though it was sketchy on details. Seems that four teenage boys, trespassing on the grounds of the bowl, which were cordoned off and identified as not to be encroached upon, had gotten themselves trapped at the bottom of it. Who knows how long they would have been down there, Pete thought, if a man had not heard their cries of "help!" and summoned Auburn Fire Rescue to the scene.

The boys were extricated with ropes and pulleys, as stranded cliff climbers at Purgatory Chasm in Sutton would have been, admonished for their foolhardiness and told "stay out of Auburn. Don't come back."

Pete turned the page and then flipped back to reread the story.

"Tommy Jankowski, Travis Nolan, Jerry Conrad and DJ Nash," he said.

"It has to be."

III

DJ was hanging out with little sis Kate in her bedroom, next to his, when Sgt. Langhorne of the Northbridge PD came calling. Pete had become accustomed to the sound of the doorbell and the sight of flashing lights in front of the house, at all hours. They always caused him to jump. They always had a sinister feel to them. They were different than they would have been if Pete's friend Harry Berkowitz had stopped by to drop off a CD from his "Days of Vinyl" show on community television, or if Suzanne Gosselin from across the street had come over to show off an abused dog she had picked up from a shelter and was nursing back to health. DJ and Kate were familiar to the NPD even before DJ busted up the front end of Pete and Mary Lou's Ford Tempo taking the curve in front of the post office too fast and Kate smashed her mouth into the steering wheel of her Mazda when she drove off the road on Linwood Ave. and had to have her teeth straightened with braces.

Both under the influence, in each incident.

"Sorry, Pete," Sgt. Langhorne said. "I have to take DJ in for violating probation."

In a department that prided itself on compassion, in writing warnings for traffic infractions instead of citations, Dick Langhorne stood out as the local police force's poster boy for looking the other way. Pete recalled the time he was driving hurriedly along Sutton St. heading toward Worcester when Sg. Langhorne pulled him over.

"You were doing 45 in a 30, Pete," he said. "Slow it down a little."

Pete knew that he had earned his share of brownie points with a weekly police log in his newspaper and with frequent articles praising the work of the NPD, often at the request of Chief Alan Pendleton. He'd done stories about a new hire, an officer working with Mothers Against Drunk Driving to spread the word in the schools about the ruinous effects of alcohol, a training session at the shooting range, a patrolman being promoted to sergeant.

There was no mention of these but Pete understood that they counted for something.

Pete led Sgt. Langhorne upstairs.

The sergeant's graying hair and benevolent countenance gave him a grandfatherly air.

He spoke quietly to DJ.

Then he turned to Pete.

"I won't put the cuffs on him, Pete." he said.

"There's no need for that."

CHAPTER TWELVE

'THEN AGAIN, I NEVER REALLY LOST HER'

The Nash children were Pete's pride and joy. A lot of people did not understand why, given the worry their travails had caused him. When questioned about this he was in the habit of responding "I love them more than I hate their occasional stumbles, and the frustration I feel in not being able to help them more."

Left unsaid was his certainty that Maddie, DJ and Kate had tripped in large part because of the compromised position he had put them in. A heaviness lay on his heart, knowing that he was at least marginally responsible for the issues they had encountered; and were still dealing with more than three decades after the relocation.

He took special pleasure in the woman Maddie had become in middle age. Behind his eldest daughter was her bold denunciation as a timid teenager of the course he had chosen for the family, which had placed her very life in jeopardy; financial problems; health woes, which had led to a brief reliance on pills to cope; an incident at the senior living facility in Auburn where she worked involving the theft of medications in a moment of weakness that could have resulted in serious time behind bars; marital strife; and finally the diagnosis of pancreatic cancer that loomed as a death sentence for Claude.

Pete had stood with her in Dudley District Court when she took out a restraining order on her husband, forcing him to move in with his parents until it was rescinded and she and Claude were together again. He had seen then, when she broke down, shaking and sobbing, how delicate she was. He had stood with her and Claude again at Worcester District Court during the weeks it took her meds' case to wind its way through the system, listening, saying to her "don't talk like that" when, in contemplating the outcome she might face, she said "I don't care, I just want this to be over."

Pete hugged Maddie when an attorney friend of Claude's, working with the DA's office, obtained a year's probation for her. It was a reprieve neither of them saw coming. Now, with her fiftieth birthday approaching, she had righted herself and had much to be thankful for despite Claude's deteriorating condition.

Theirs was a marriage that would not have happened except for Claude Lucier's relentless pursuit of Maddie, even to the point of living out of his car while trying to stay within sight of her, even while trying to wrest her away from a rival suitor—Jamie Smith—she was committed to at the time.

Pete initially saw Claude's doggedness as a quality to be admired. Pete embraced it. He recognized in Claude, the son of Julien and Estelle Lucier of Worcester and then Sturbridge, the same determination he had apparently exhibited on the basketball court as a member of a winning Worcester Voke team—during his high school years. Pete had indeed felt it, during pickup games in the backyard of Claude and Maddie's house on Arthur St. in Worcester before they moved to Oxford: Claude's bulk against him, Claude's elbows digging into his ribs, Claude's fierce drive to push past defenders and get to the hoop.

It wasn't until much later that this attribute took on a different, more menacing connotation. "It's as if he wants to control her, possess her," Pete thought, in Claude's objections to the places where Maddie chose to work and to the friendships she made. As Claude's illness worsened, his need to confront Maddie, to challenge her, criticize her, increased. His proclivity for sudden rages that turned to verbal abuse left Maddie on edge. Her attempts to ignore the insults he hurled at her when anger got the best of him only incensed him that much more. It was an untenable situation and it was too late for it to get any better.

Their marriage had a definite up side, however.

In Cassandra, Jocelyn and Mitchell, they had fulfilled their dream of parenthood and brought into the world three individuals whose striving for success gave them comfort—and a sense of accomplishment. Cassandra was working as a financial advisor in Worcester, Jocelyn for a company in Auburn that manufactured uniforms and work gear, and Mitchell was studying mechanical engineering at Wentworth Institute of Technology in Boston.

In the home set on a hill that she and Claude had owned and occupied since leaving Worcester, Maddie had found a reason to believe that the future held promise. The steep remnants of what had passed for a driveway, which had been such a source of irritation to her and to visitors, was repaved and the farmer's porch on the front that she had envisioned as a crowning touch was being built. This was the home that she was constantly improving with paint and carpet and tile and shelving and photos and wall mountings. Whatever she put on the wall championed the importance of family and love. She displayed these with a designer's eye for tasteful expression.

In her jobs cashiering at the local supermarket and the dollar store, situated in the same plaza just two miles from her home, she had found the satisfaction that had allowed her to become more assertive. She became friends with a woman with whom she could laugh and cry and share confidences over coffee.

In Alexandra she had found the niece whose scars from childhood she could soothe, who she could counsel and uphold as she would one of her own daughters. In Alex's newborns Tyler and Ned she had found the infants who would infuse her life with new meaning.

In Weight Watchers she had found the key to the svelte figure that would enhance her natural beauty and let her move ahead knowing that she was a woman who mattered.

Best of all, in her adoration of her father she had found the forgiveness that had enabled the two of them to appreciate their mutual zest for life in all of its cruelty and all of its grandeur.

Pete could not have asked for a better outcome than knowing he had won Maddie back.

"Then again, I never really lost her," he thought.

CHAPTER THIRTEEN

LEVITY, LIGHTENING THE WEIGHT OF DESPAIR

DJ in his forty-fifth year and after much exertion had seemingly put the scourge of alcoholism behind him. "This I am reasonably sure of," Pete would tell himself, convinced that it was true.

He wished he could proclaim in sixty-point Bodoni or Helvetica headlines word that DJ had conquered his fiercest foe. He wondered if anyone but DJ, Maddie, Kate and himself fully grasped the significance of this achievement. He questioned whether anyone but a handful of loved ones understood the resolve it must have taken for DJ to beat back once and for all the temptation to pick up again.

Elusive sobriety was DJ's at last, Pete hoped. Gram Jenkins and Gram Nash would pat him on the head and say "good job, grandson." Christ, whose teachings DJ followed so fervently in his daily Bible readings, would whisper in his ear "well done, good and faithful servant."

"If only," Pete thought, "this would translate into acceptance of DJ by those who would never let go of their disdain for him for his prior slips. They just don't get how hard it has been for him to summon the will to put the bottle down for good."

Pete thought of DJ feeling shunned at a memorial gathering for his Uncle Lucas in East Rochester, New York a few summers before; feeling ignored by cousins he was once close to but now rarely saw—whose success in the workplace contributed to the feeling of inferiority that was already part of the baggage he carried around. How he looked forward to renewing his ties too with Sally Rae, his beloved "Cuda," the aunt who had always kept him close, who he had always counted on to treat him as a nephew she considered to be especially deserving of her attention. Maybe Sally Rae saw vulnerability that others missed?

It was hard for DJ to accept that Sally Rae's preoccupation with the death of her husband, and with catering to those present for the "celebration of life" she was hosting, couldn't give him the time he thought he was due. "But,"

Pete thought, "this is so typical of him. He is easily offended, even when others don't mean any harm. He reads into people's attitudes slights that aren't there."

Sally Rae—Cuda—loved DJ no less than she ever had. "I will explain that to him," Pete thought. "He has to know she is no less interested in him."

In Sally Rae's living room that Saturday evening, Pete listened in, his ears thumping with gratitude, as Joe Sweeney talked back and forth with DJ for half an hour. Joe, the brother-in-law Pete had shared so many conversations with about baseball and the Yankees. Joe and Pete could wile away whole afternoons, enjoying each other's company. Now Joe was making sure DJ felt welcomed.

Bending to catch the drift of the talk between the two of them, Pete said to himself "only Joe Sweeney would go out of his way to let DJ vent, as he is wont to do. Only Joe would try and bolster his spirits, tell him his dream of owning a landscaping company could in fact come true."

Pete knew Joe to be one kindhearted uncle. Still, what it must have taken for Joe Sweeney to give DJ his undivided attention.

It was a moment Pete would never forget.

II

For many years, DJ had blamed Pete for the ruinous path his life had taken, even while heralding him as "the greatest dad." In one breath there would be a comment, a text message or a voice mail excoriating Pete for placing career over family. In the next there would be high praise for the effort Pete exerted in maintaining the safety net that caught DJ every time he was in danger of falling. There was appreciation too, from DJ, for Pete's willingness to step up in the same way for his sisters, for Mary Lou, and for others.

This phenomenon, DJ spouting, DJ extolling, went on and on until finally he started raising the possibility that his need for scripts to stave off despondency, insomnia, "racing thoughts" and "creepy crawly things on my legs" could be traced back to a head injury he had suffered when he was six.

Suddenly Pete was no longer the culprit. It was the spill DJ had taken.

Pete, Mary Lou and the children were on a picnic in the country with Dick and Gretchen Boardman when DJ was thrown off a spinning tilt-a-whirl, the same kind Pete had ridden standing up—and often without hanging onto the handles—at West Endicott Park when he was young. DJ had hit his head on a rock. Scrambling to his aid, Dick, Pete and Mary Lou had wrapped his head with a towel, packed him into the car and raced to Ideal Hospital—ten miles away.

It took fourteen stitches to close the gash.

Of late DJ with a thin scar about three inches long on top of his scalp as a remnant of the incident had been saying to Pete "we need to get my medical records from Dr. Giordano's office in Endicott, dad. Do you think he's still practicing?" Or "I am going to have a brain scan at St. V's or Memorial. I'm sure it will show something's not right."

Nothing came of this. Between themselves Pete and Mary Lou dismissed the notion that anything but DJ's long history of using was responsible for the various ailments he now suffered.

They didn't need a pediatrician or a PCP to tell them what they knew in their hearts.

DJ was an addict. Yes, he had loosed the restraints the disease imposed on him. But symptoms still persisted. Would he ever be completely free of them?

III

DJ enjoyed sharing with Pete amusing moments that he knew his father would appreciate. Being able to laugh after all of the summonses to court that he had to answer to for violating the custodial agreement with his former wife provided both of them with the sense of relief they needed. Unlike DJ and Pete, Kylie Miller (she had reclaimed her maiden name) appeared to relish the snare she had put him in. The interminable minutes and hours he would have to spend in court, fuming, while she paraded about the third-floor concourse in her pink pants suit and bleached blond hair left him in an ugly mood.

How Pete and DJ hated going back to Worcester District Court time after time! Pete, especially. "I don't belong here," he would tell himself while standing against a wall reading *The Adventures of Huckleberry Finn* or *Of Mice and Men* and looking on with disgust at the couples shouting at each other across the marble floor in an attempt to settle a domestic dispute.

"I was here with Gov. Patrick and all of the other dignitaries for the grand opening of this multimillion-dollar palace," Pete thought. "I wrote about it! What will people think when they see me here?" Invariably at that moment an attorney Pete knew who also served on the Worcester City Council would walk by, recognize Pete and say, sarcastically, "another day in paradise." Ratifying for Pete the shabbiness of what transpired in the halls of the place, its shimmer notwithstanding.

But there was no getting around it. Capitalizing on her bitterness over DJ's drinking, which persisted long after they split—and which enabled her to cast him as a most unsavory character to anyone who would listen—Kylie with the assistance of her legal counsel duped him into signing a document that allowed him only supervised visits on a limited basis with his two younger daughters until they were twenty-three. This was not even the most demeaning blow. That would be Kylie and Amory passing DJ as he pushed a cart full of groceries from the pantry and Kylie saying with abundant smugness "look, honey, there's your father." Hearing DJ tell this, Pete could sense the sting from which he smarted.

The monitoring of DJ's time with his girls fell to Pete by default. In his sixties and seventies he would curse his misfortune in being saddled with the obligation of making sure DJ got to where he was supposed to, or wanted to, be. When DJ was semi-homeless this could involve retrieving him from Main Street in Worcester at ten o'clock at night (as Mary Lou picked at her hands in her recliner, which was a habit she had developed when upset or worried), from his friend Johnny's house in Webster Square, from the PIP shelter in Main South or from the Burger King at Kelley Square. At such times Pete had to restrain himself from lashing out at the injustice of the arrangement.

As a counter to the friction that boiled in him whenever his cell phone rang and the voice on the other end said "dad, can you come and get me," Pete liked that DJ could share hilarious incidents with him. These did not come often but they left both of them in a better mood.

IV

"Dad," DJ said one afternoon on I-290 as they left Worcester for Oxford, "did I ever tell you about the time that cheapo lard ass Pat Michaels caught me badmouthing him?"

Pete knew that DJ had been undervalued during the two years he worked as a foreman with Michaels' landscaping company. This didn't surprise him. Pat Michaels had been born into wealth as a child of friends of Pete's who owned nursing homes in Northbridge and Westborough. Daniel and Dottie Michaels were two of the most admirable people Pete associated with as a journalist; they were solid citizens and conscientious in the care they provided to the aging and the infirm. Their nursing homes, at least then, were models of efficiency.

By handing Pat Michaels everything he wanted including the money he needed to expand a small mowing business into a full-service lawn and property-maintenance firm, however, they had turned their spoiled brat of a son into an ogre.

"I had the Guatemalans in the truck with me," DJ said. "That was when I was still driving. You know I always treated them right, on the job. Made sure they got water and lunch breaks. Joked around with them. Listened to them gripe about the menial wages Michaels paid them. They knew I disliked him as much as they did.

"We were headed to a cleanup a couple of towns over from the barn in Uxbridge. They were jabbering in broken English about the boss. I was getting a kick out of their complaints, because of the salty language they used—our tongue and theirs. They were all worked up.

"All of a sudden I began banging my free hand on the dashboard. Like I was agreeing with them about what they said.

"That fat fuck," I said. "I'll knock him flat one of these days!

"I had them in stitches, dad. They were loving it.

"I had no sooner gotten the words out than my cell phone starts ringing. It was Pat Michaels. He says to me, 'the CB is on here!' Everyone back at the shop had heard what I said!

"I says to him, 'aaannnddd?' Like, what did I care?

"Michaels hangs up. He calls right back, though. 'We'll talk about this tonight,' he says.

"When we got back, he was gone for the day."

V

Pete was reassured whenever DJ was able to see the lighter side of things, this way. It suggested to Pete that all was not lost. It also appealed to Pete's inclination to laugh at many of life's inane moments. He had been doing this for as long as he could recall, his funny bone reverberating like a tuning fork whenever anything struck him as absurd. DJ knew this and so he looked for chances to yank stories from his memory bank just for the rise they would get from Pete.

Much of what transpired at the "sober house" in Oxford where DJ had been living for the past three years, for instance, was too ugly for words. The riffraff came and went, leaving in their wake, for DJ to mull, thoughts of friendships made and other thoughts of "so long, not at all sorry to see you go."

Rick from the North Shore had done time for armed robbery but no one would have suspected that. Rick was courteous and well-mannered, always addressed Pete as "Mr. Nash." He was soft-spoken almost to the point of reticence, displaying in his demeanor—Pete concluded—remorse for the great errors of his youth. Rick was on the rebound, trying to walk the straight and narrow, projecting a certain contentment in having driven into submission the urges that had dictated his former life.

DJ looked upon Rick as a brother. They were about the same age, DJ the taller and fairer complexioned of the two, Rick swarthier and stockier. They enjoyed providing each other with cigarettes, exchanging small talk about the weather, the Red Sox, politics and world events. Pete for his part saw Rick as the anchor who would help keep DJ grounded. There was nothing threatening about Rick. In his cutoff jeans, flip flops and Metallica T-shirt, he was the essence of go-along-to-get-along. Like DJ, he was not looking for drama or trouble.

Rick talked often about finding his own place. He finally did, latching onto a second-floor flat in neighboring Webster. A month later, he overdosed.

He lay dead for two days before the landlord found him.

"You gave him the pills that killed him!" Nancy said. DJ had gotten close to Nancy through AA but their friendship had soured. DJ did not mind that Nancy and Rick had become close. He was happy for them. But her accusation hurt.

"I did not! I would never!" DJ said. "Rick was like family to me!"

Pete told DJ to take into account the woman Nancy was. She was a hag-like, decrepit specter with her dull graying hair knotted in a ponytail. She was consumed by bitterness toward anyone and everything. She was so handicapped by a diffidence to the plight of her fellow boarders that she proved to be ineffectual during a temporary stint as house manager.

"She is not worth getting riled up over," Pete said. "I know how you felt about Rick. That's all that matters."

DJ wrote a poem about Rick, posted it with a photo of his friend on a wall in the living room near the framed picture of the Obama inauguration. Shortly afterwards he found it leaning against the door to his room, the tacks he'd used to pin it up lying on the floor.

DJ wept for days.

VI

Carlos, who DJ liked, met the same fate as Rick; and in the same shocking fashion. Carlos left three children fatherless.

Luis up and left. Lisa did too; and Corbin. Steve, who had been homeless on the streets of Worcester until landing in Oxford, suddenly disappeared overnight. The only clue that Steve had lived at 266 Main St. for several months were the possessions he'd left behind in his room. Pete could not comprehend it. Steve had graduated from Holy Cross. He had impressed Pete as being more together than most. He had been attending the Methodist church with DJ and Pete and lobbying Pete to exert his influence on the Worcester city manager to gain support for a scheme he had concocted.

"I want the city to get behind my idea of an all-volunteer force of Samaritans," Steve said. "Formerly homeless people like me, if they are physically and mentally competent, who could be recruited to help others. They would fan out across the city, steer the down-and-out toward the services they need, end the panhandling that's going on, be the impetus for a different approach to the problem. Be part of a solution that works."

Steve made it clear to Pete that he had been a classmate of the city manager's on College Hill. He just wanted Pete to use his leverage as a newspaperman to make the approach.

Brenda was gone too. She and Loretta had battled for mastery of the house. One of their many confrontations occurred when Loretta tried to wrest the TV remote from Brenda so that she could watch "Judge Judy." Brenda hurled the device at her, raising a black eye and a lump on Loretta's forehead. Loretta took out a restraining order against her. Brenda left, content to cope as best she could in the hellhole of Pleasant St. in Worcester.

Through it all DJ had tried to maintain his equilibrium and to stay above the tumult. This wasn't easy. It was made more difficult when a man named Jug arrived. A more unsavory character could not have been found skulking on Skid Row or rummaging for scraps along the banks of the Mystic River. Pete figured Jug, whose given name was Joseph, to be in his early sixties. He was short but powerfully built and square-jawed with small but hardened hands and a countenance that suggested having taken lumps in bar fights; or maybe as a onetime welterweight boxing on the undercard at the Palladium. He spewed invective as if sucking it from a bottomless pit.

He had nasty written all over him.

Jug showed up just before Carlos died. With disparaging remarks about Carlos' Hispanic heritage and worthlessness, delivered in a loud and incessant torrent, Jug compounded DJ's grief.

"I'd like to bust his teeth," DJ seethed.

"You know that can't happen," Pete said. "No more trips to the courthouse!"

"He's nothing but a pig, a sex fiend, dad. You know what he said to Jennifer when he passed her in the hallway one day, knowing that she and I were dating? You know how insecure she is. He says 'my room, right now!' She says back 'excuse me?' As if she'd get into the sack with that creep."

There was not much about Jug to warrant laughter. Except for the part-time work he picked up as a carpenter, he lived on the loll, swallowing in liquid form from morning to night the assistance he got from the state, just as others in the house did. In the summer of 2019 three of them would hang at the back of the property in lawn chairs, bare chested, soaking up the sun, with not a care in the world, Jug with his cap turned backwards, mouthing filth about anyone who was not part of his clique. Then he would climb on the house bicycle and ride the sidewalk north toward the town center, or south toward the liquor store, pedaling the contraption with the casual air of a Parisian headed to the café or the bookstore.

DJ knew Pete would appreciate a Jug story. So he told of the night Jug, wavering recklessly as he roared back down the driveway after a turn through the neighborhood, smashed into and knocked over a charcoal grill.

"Carl saw him do it, dad," DJ said. Pete instantly conjured up an image of Carl; Carl standing on the stoop in his customary attire—a checkered flannel robe, like a character out of *One Flew Over The Cuckoo's Nest*, his hair askew, puffing on a cigarette, offering to Pete a courtesy hello in recognition of his arrival in the Nissan. Pete had decided that Carl was the most innocuous creature this side of Big Bird. At least until DJ told him that Carl kept a pistol in his room, and that he had been warned about going outside to shoot at rabbits and squirrels.

"When Carl saw this, when he saw Jug and the bicycle splattered on the ground, coals all around them, he started running toward Jug. He screams 'I just bought that grill. It's brand new! I'll destroy your ass, you no-good-for-nothing bastard!'"

Pete chuckled.

"I would love to have seen that," Pete said. "Carl? Carl who looks like a patient from a mental hospital? Who only communicates with me by a feeble wave of his hand?

"I just can't picture it."

CHAPTER FOURTEEN
HELLO, MARY LOU

Before Mary Lou was a Nash she was a Jenkins. She had remained a Jenkins in numerous ways all her life. She did not shed the identity that the name carried, as her father's daughter. She reveled in it and in fact conducted herself in a manner that would have prompted Albert Jenkins to bestow accolades on her—had he not passed in 1990.

From the outset of her marriage, Mary Lou was guided in her decision making, movements and interests by the same instincts that had been Pa Jenkins' call to action. She never veered from this path. Her respect for him was as profound as a student's for a revered professor or mentor.

Like her father, who she always referred to as "daddy" in a tone that was reverential across the spectrum of its two syllables, she was level-headed. She rarely behaved foolishly, or impishly—like Pete. The closest Pete had ever known her to come to irresponsibility was when all inhibitions were cast aside in the back seat of her VW bug beneath the stars with the top down, or on the sofa or the stoop of her parents' home; when she and Pete were ravenous for each other. Pete would smile long afterwards in remembering Grace standing at the top of the stairs as he and Mary Lou necked furiously, Grace fearful of taking another step toward them, Grace whispering loud enough for Mary Lou to hear "don't you think it's time you came to bed, honey?"

"Soon, mama," Mary Lou would say. "We've got Johnny Mathis on."

It was not in Mary Lou's nature to approach a matter with anything but the common sense she was born with, fortified as she grew by observing Pa's irrefutable logic at work. She watched him, learned from him, put the lessons he taught in sound judgment to good use as a mother and wife. Life was serious business, meant to be taken seriously. There was no room for faulty, misguided, shallow thinking.

She wore no jewelry except for a necklace or brooch that Pete would buy for her; a dab of lipstick and eye shadow. These on the rarest of occasions, when she and Pete went out. Pete could not recall a time when Mary Lou put on earrings. Or a bracelet. She was the most unusual woman Pete had ever known in this regard, in her rejection too of turtleneck sweaters.

"I hate anything around my neck," she would say. "I don't like that."

When they were young and Mary Lou was slim Pete often wished he could see her in tight jeans, a halter top and black boots. This wasn't her style. She was prim and proper. She was not given to outlandishness.

She was, however, keen on dispensing advice she thought he needed to hear.

He appreciated this about her too, even if it rankled him when first uttered.

"I wish you would use the coverlet we got on the arms of the recliner," she would say to Pete. They had purchased the eight hundred-dollar electrically powered chair for him several months before at the neighborhood furniture store.

"I'm going to rock away my golden years in it!" Pete would tell his children and grandkids when they came by. In the scorching heat of the summer of 2019, however, he had fallen into the habit of letting the coverlet scrunch up into a ball as he got in and out of the chair.

"I try," Pete said. "It won't stay in place. Or I forget."

"Well, don't," Mary Lou scolded. "We don't need your sweaty, yukky arms and legs all over it, after you've been mowing the lawn. We want it to last!"

Pete would sulk for a moment as he straightened the coverlet up but then think "this is the woman I know and love. Who keeps me from going off half-cocked.

"The same woman," he would think, "who is so careful about balancing her checkbook, who makes sure the young ones have sunscreen on at the beach, who points out to me even before I've noticed that the tires on the car are soft, who cautions me about a pothole when I am distracted, who asks me to tie up the hydrangea next to the house so that its branches and leaves aren't coming into contact with the air conditioner sticking out of our bedroom window, who pays bills ahead of the time they're due, who writes notes to herself as reminders of things that need to be done, who fills the watering can after giving the fuchsia plant Maddie buys her for Mother's Day and her birthday every year a drink."

"It's better to have a full can of warm water to start with, tomorrow," she would say.

"If Pa Jenkins was around, he would have said the same thing," Pete thought.

II

Like her father, Mary Lou was wary of the kind of goofiness—slapstick and otherwise—that Pete found so intoxicating. This extended to responding not always with laughter but with reservation to her husband's own persistent efforts to get her to loosen up. This often would not produce the effect Pete was looking for.

One day Pete received a text from his brother. "It's Roy…" the message read…"this is my new cell number." Staring at the ten digits Roy was now using, Pete realized he would have to go into the Contacts list on his own cell phone to keep Roy "current."

He couldn't resist the chance to be coy about it.

"Are you on the lam or something? LOL," Pete replied.

"Very funny," came the response. "Not on the lam, but I needed a new phone."

After reading the texts, Mary Lou looked at Pete, smiled, and said "but he wouldn't be giving out the number if he's on the lam!"

"Such powers of deduction!" Pete thought. He was disappointed that Mary Lou hadn't gotten it, but amazed as well by how her brain worked—keen as a scientist's, or her dad's.

Pete liked trying to make Mary Lou laugh. He persisted, though many attempts had missed the mark.

"Hey, hon, did you read 'Blondie' today?" he asked one afternoon from the recliner. He was already consumed by riotous giggling, certain that this would be the only tipoff needed to stir in her the same exhilaration he was feeling.

"I think so, I can't remember what it was about though," she answered from the kitchen sink, where she was peeling peaches for a cobbler.

"Dagwood drops a note in the company Suggestion box and it's a shredder!" Pete said, his body convulsing. "Mr. Dithers' doing of course!"

Pete thought as he said this that his boisterous cackling at the hilarity of the Dean Young and John Marshall comic panel would strip the paint off the ceiling.

He felt a rush of pleasure when Mary Lou paused what she was doing to reply.

He could see her, the blade of the knife suspended over the piece of fruit, stopping long enough to look out the kitchen window and maybe say to herself "that's my Pete."

"Yeah, that's a good one!" she shouted back.

"That's *it* ?" Pete thought. "Come on, girl!"

III

What had drawn Pete to Mary Lou wasn't as it turned out what he found most alluring about her to begin with.

Initially, for both of them, the attraction was the all-consuming physical urges that were raging; the yearning to get it on whenever and wherever the spirit moved them and convention be damned.

Both were on the rebound, Pete from an as-yet nonsexual liaison with a homely girl from the Binghamton General side of the city who he'd met at the newspaper office, Mary Lou from one with a volatile suitor from New Jersey named "Howie." Pete broke things off when the sight of "Anita's" father in a state of perpetual inebriation on the sofa became more than he could stand. Pete couldn't tolerate lackadaisical. Mary Lou did the same when Howie pulled a switchblade on her brother-in-law Lucas in the driveway of Lucas and Sally Rae's apartment.

That first night, at the bar on the North Side of Endicott, on a blind date arranged by Lucas and Sally Rae, Pete was not sure what to make of Mary Lou. She was not what he had envisioned as "the catch." He had in mind a blond, not a woman with a full head of hair black as ink (which, like her dad's, would not go anywhere near completely gray even in her mid-seventies—or thin out to mere strands one could see through).

Pete hadn't even really been in the market. At twenty-two, as one of the youngest sports editors of a daily newspaper in the country, he was satisfied with the games that garnered most of his attention. He thought of himself as unencumbered—without restraints. He was not burdened by alliances with a woman that would have pulled him away from the livelihood that carried with it prime views from the press box or from courtside that Yankees announcer "Red" Barber would refer to in a book he wrote as the best of all possible perches: "the catbird seat."

Pete had told his brothers there was no way he would wed before the age of thirty. He was having too much fun. Why spoil the good times by getting tied down? He was running free. Basketball at the Y, a cigar in his mouth at work.

Before meeting Mary Lou, Pete had immersed himself in the life of a bachelor, running with his sports-writing pal John Leykam, drinking, carousing, smoking White Owls, lapping up complimentary passes to the Army-Navy game in Philadelphia, boxing matches at the CYC in Scranton, the U.S. Open at Baltusrol or Winged Foot, the Mets versus the Cubs at Shea Stadium.

"What could possibly surpass the sight of Dave 'King Kong' Kingman blasting a home run clean out of the ballpark?" Pete asked himself. "Watching it silhouetted against a dark summer sky, a white speck lifting like a rocket from the launch pad at Cape Canaveral, the goose bumps on my arms?"

Leykam, from well-heeled New Rochelle, Iona College-educated, would take Pete into the city from Binghamton, weekends, show him how to ride the subway, arrange dates for him, introduce him to fellow "Gaels" at taverns where "Johnny boy" was instantly recognized and greeted as a soldier returning from war would be, escort him to Gatsby-like parties at mansions sprinkled throughout northern New Jersey.

John Leykam would in fact accompany Pete "on assignment" to Ft. Lauderdale for spring training in March of 1968, mere months after Pete and Mary Lou had met. Pete had been dispatched to Florida by the *Sun-Bulletin's* managing editor to report on the exploits of raw-boned young pitchers and catchers and outfielders and infielders who were trying to "stick" with the Yankees' Class AA farm team: the Binghamton Triplets. Each afternoon after leaving the big club's complex Pete would hammer out five to eight hundred words on the portable typewriter Beatrice Nash had bought for him and telephone in the piece to George Clements for publication the next morning.

That accomplished, Pete and John would grab dinner, Pete with the meal money Clements had allocated to him, and head to a strip club in nearby Hollywood. It was a pastime they had taken up back in Binghamton. It was what unattached guys their age did, Pete reasoned, ignoring for the time being his strict Baptist upbringing at the hands of his maternal grandmother. They drank cheap beer by the bottle, eyed "fast girls" through a smoky haze as the women danced in nothing but a G-string, stayed for last call at 2:00 a.m., slept late.

Pete would not have traded those nights for an autographed Ernie Banks, Stan Musial or Willie Mays rookie card.

But then there was Mary Lou, waiting in Vestal for his return and the resumption of their budding romance.

"Baby, you've been on my mind," Pete would think.

IV

Pete knew even while drinking fresh-squeezed orange juice in a booth in a restaurant on East Broward Boulevard mornings before he and John headed to the ballpark, even while enjoying his first taste of Florida's glorious rays and the cute, flirtatious waitresses in their brightly colored aprons who delivered the beverage, even as he elevated himself in his speculative moments to the stature of an Arthur Daley of *The New York Times* or a Dick Young of the *Daily News*, that he would be asking Mary Lou to be his bride.

His week in the Sunshine State would be one of his last as a free man. He would wait at the end of the aisle at the Methodist church in Vestal for Mary Lou to walk to him on Pa's arm on a steamy day in early September, a little over a month before his twenty-third birthday. They would honeymoon in Provincetown, neither with an inkling then that they would eventually wind up in Massachusetts.

That Mary Lou was an exact opposite of his dream girl would ultimately prove to be what was most endearing about her. She was not what he even would have identified to John or any of his friends, or his brothers, as "a chick." She was, he quickly determined, not a tramp but a lady. He would forever think of her as that, as the years flowed past. She was refined, averse to swear words, modest in her wardrobe save for her accent on the color red, undemonstrative in public, meticulous in her personal hygiene, deeply attentive to the teachings found in Scripture, ardently devoted to the concept of matrimony and motherhood.

There would be six pregnancies and three miscarriages. The bond between Pete and Mary Lou would remain firm and indeed strengthen with these and other tests of their will. Maddie, DJ and Kate brought to them the children they both wanted; the babies who would enrich their lives and yes the adults whose struggles would become a source of concern and occasionally exasperation but never a cause for complete alienation.

Mary Lou proved to be more than Pete could have hoped for in a soulmate. As an LPN, the caring mentality she brought to patients in the hospital and to the elderly in the senior-living residences in which she worked, before retiring, manifested itself as well in the role she took on from the outset as a homemaker.

Pete was appreciative even if he didn't always show it. The woman who nursed and disciplined the children, who would take on the task of cooking dinner every night of the week—and deriving satisfaction from it—who baked bread and pies, who canned tomatoes Pete grew in the garden, who sewed torn garments, who crocheted lovely afghans (most of which she gave away), who exhibited unequivocal affection for him despite his whimsical leanings, who drew such strength from the grandchildren and great grandkids: not in his wildest imaginings had he foreseen "this Vestal girl" as his partner for all-time.

By the time Mary Lou's health began to deteriorate, her hearing loss compounded by the aftereffects of a broken ankle she suffered at Wells Beach in 2009, knee issues and the nag of arthritis, her routine had changed. She stayed up late, reading. She gave her mornings over to the newspaper and word puzzle in it. She allocated her afternoons to conversing by telephone with Sarah, napping and catching up on TV shows she had recorded: DIY programs, instructional videos on The Food Network, how-to half-hour spots from Ina Garten and Martha Stewart, documentaries about Alaska, elephants and whales.

They settled into a pattern. Dinner at six o'clock, the evening news, "Wheel of Fortune" and "Jeopardy," a Red Sox game, shows she had taped that they liked: "Parenthood," "The Blacklist," "Bluebloods," "This Is Us," "Law & Order-SVU."

The children and grandchildren thought of Pete and Mary Lou's union as the perfect marriage. Amory, DJ's middle child, thought of them as "cute." In the important regards their marriage was something everyone admired. Maddie, DJ and Kate would see the hand holding or Pete's arm around Mary Lou on the porch swing, the impromptu pecks on the cheek back and forth, "babe" this and "babe" that, Mary Lou laying out a home-cooked meal and Pete doing the dishes afterwards as was their arrangement, the greeting cards they exchanged with tender notes penned inside and they would say to themselves "mom and dad, Nana and Pop, they are the exception."

Any frictions that existed lay unexposed to the naked eye, like the rocks that are so prevalent in Massachusetts, that Pete's shovel would strike with a metallic echo within seconds when he was digging a hole to sink a post into or turning over the soil before planting tulips, hibiscus, onions or peppers.

Knowing what they knew, Maddie, DJ and Kate still only witnessed a fraction of the commiseration that kept the branch of the tree that Pete and Mary Lou shared from snapping in two. They were not present most of the time for the gentle picking and prodding he subjected her to as a sign of his love for her; or her equally playful retorts. They would not necessarily be privy to a mild criticism or reprimand she offered up, if, for instance, he neglected to wipe mustard from the butter knife before putting it in the dishwasher so it wouldn't rust; or his immediate comeback: "well, speaking of complaints, I've got one: you leave the sticky labels on fruit on the edge of the kitchen sink and I can't get them off for weeks on end!"—said with a smile. They would not then see Mary Lou remove several more of these from a pear in a bowl on the counter and place them on top of the ones already there. This was the gentle retaliation she was capable of, that made them both laugh.

Theirs was the sort of repartee they had fine-tuned over time, as Pa Jenkins would have tinkered and improved the sound of the engine of the Impalas he liked to drive.

They were not around either one morning when Pete, feeling "too big for his britches," as Beatrice Nash would have put it, his ego inflated by a lifetime in journalism and some recent accomplishment or recognition, said to Mary Lou, "when I die I want a big obit for all my friends to see."

Mary Lou looked up from the newspaper and without a blink of the eye said "you'll get five words: Pete died, forget about it."

CHAPTER FIFTEEN
THE WAY WE WERE

July 2019

A tradition had developed; a ritual, not unlike the running of the bulls, an Easter egg hunt on the lawn of the White House or the class reunions that were now occurring less frequently back in Endicott and with fewer of Pete Nash's fellow grads of 1963 attending.

Every year, around Christmastime, Maddie, DJ and Kate would break out a family videocassette that Maddie's Claude had arranged to have made and slip it into the tape player in Pete and Mary Lou's living room. Those who could be present for the viewing would sit or sprawl in front of the TV in anticipation of "the life of the Nash's" flashing across the screen, with musical accompaniment from the 1970s and 1980s as background.

Maddie, DJ and Kate had begun the exercise as a way of reaffirming their love for their parents and for each other. It was also an effort on their part to share with their own then-young children (now numbering seven) the pride they felt in vivid memories of happy days gone by.

Their objective was obvious to Pete. "This is what family is all about," they were saying to their children. "Remember this as you grow and mature and marry and have kids. Be the Nash's. Stay united, no matter what (similarly, years later, Maddie and Alexandra would suggest family gatherings on Saturday afternoons at Pete and Mary Lou's home and these too became a regular thing, with the provision of food discussed ahead of time and turns taken in bringing it).

Feeling the excitement in the room when the video was inserted, seeing the radiance on the faces of Maddie, DJ and Kate, savoring the elation they expressed in maintaining a cherished custom, Pete thought of the summer lawn parties of his youth that were organized in celebration of his paternal grandfather's birthday. These took place at Horace Nash Sr. and Lillian's "EJ" home on Jennings Street in West Endicott and were not to be missed.

Pete had never experienced anything like them before—or since. At six and eight and ten and thirteen, he understood them to be the social happening of the season. He thought about them with great expectation weeks in advance. He pictured his aunts and uncles arriving in their pastel blouses and white shorts and short-sleeved shirts, toting bowls of potato salad and two-liter bottles of Coca-Cola and Italian bread from Roma's Bakery. Into each slice of bread they would slip charcoal-roasted lamb "spiedies" that had been sizzling on skewers on the grill. The spiedies were marinated in a special sauce concocted by Pete's Uncle Stu, with spearmint leaves added as the crowning touch for flavor.

His penchant for exhibitionism and deviltry made Gramps Nash the star attraction but for Pete it was the chance to frolic with his cousins. This did not come often enough. They fanned out for impromptu games of hide and seek or dodgeball or badminton while the adults commiserated over glasses of iced tea and lemonade, Pete taking for granted that it would always be this way with Stu and Honey's Jack and Dan, Ray and Hazel's Gary, Nancy and Larry (Suzie, too, when she came along), Bob and Alberta's Sandy, Bobby, Roberta and Sharon, Bun and Harriett's Carol and Joyce, and his brothers.

It could not last forever. It had to end sometime and it did, with the death of Grampa Nash. In the years that followed, Pete's cousins started to drop away as age exacted its toll. Others he lost touch with.

At the wedding of his nephew James in Waterloo, New York in June of 2019, a niece of Pete's who had heard about "those family get-togethers" around the Fourth of July proposed to him that the two of them plan a re-enactment. It pleased Pete that Amy Nash, the daughter of his youngest brother Myles and sister of James, spry and spirited—a marathoner who confided to him that she was going to "run Boston" in the spring of 2020 if she could post a mandatory qualifying time in Washington State in September—was interested enough to suggest such an assembly. She had heard the stories. They had piqued her desire.

Pete was sure it wouldn't happen, however. He was glad that some remnants of yesteryear had been held onto. After much exertion, after much trial and error, for instance, Roy Nash had finally mastered Beatrice Nash's recipes for cinnamon rolls and cream puffs.

But Pete knew Amy's proposal wouldn't go far.

Thinking now of Grampa Nash, the West Endicott blowouts and his cousins, Pete realized, consumed by regret, that the video had not been viewed in a while. It lay in a drawer in the TV stand along with old movies Pete and Mary Lou hadn't watched in years, including *The Way We Were* which was their first pick in a pinch—when Robert Redford and Barbra Streisand were, like Pete and Mary Lou once, oblivious to Father Time.

"I cannot remember the last time we watched the family video," Pete thought.

"We don't even have a tape player these days."

CHAPTER SIXTEEN
A COLD HARD REALITY

One morning Pete wrote this in his journal: *With age comes a certain melancholy, even for someone as spirit-filled as myself. An awareness that one's months, weeks, days are dwindling down to a precious few. As was noted in a song I heard on the radio: "Time swallows everything."*

He was feeling reflective and a little low. He had been contemplating his own death for...how long now? He wondered if his contemporaries, his school-days' pal Bill Thayer in Springfield and others of their generation, spent an inordinate amount of their waking hours doing the same. Bill suffered from an assortment of ills including failing vision. Pete thought, "isn't it unhealthy to be absorbed in so macabre a subject? Does something others hear or read trigger in them, as it does in me, an instantaneous meditation on our pending exit from 'this mortal coil?'"

Suddenly Pete would be seized by a panic attack that even the comforting words contained in the Scriptures or in the sermons of Pastor Barry in Oxford could not alleviate. But then he would say to himself "shake it off! The end of days for you is no different than for most others! What gives you the notion that you are special and should be exempt from the outcome that awaits all of us?"

Then he would come across a reminder that aging is nothing to fear, as in the Irish proverb that showed up in a bulletin from the local senior center that he received in the mail each month:

Do not resent growing old. Many are denied the privilege.

He had been listening recently to Willie Nelson singing about being "the last man standing," Willie grieving at the loss, too soon, of friends like Merle Haggard. Willie asserting, in one breath, that he didn't want to be the only one left, and in the next, "then again maybe I do."

"I know that feeling!" Pete would tell himself. "I can't explain why so many people I have known and cared for, relatives and acquaintances, have been taken and I am still here. But I would be lying if I said I wasn't grateful for every additional day I'm given, though I miss them all so much."

Then his thoughts would turn to Maddie, DJ and Kate. All of them in their forties, all of them having not yet slipped the noose that had been placed around their necks—by him, Pete Nash, orchestrator of The Move and the woes it had wrought.

The possibility of their premature demise surpassed in magnitude even the certainty of his own.

II

Pete's education on the scourge of alcohol and drugs had reached a pinnacle of sorts on a Saturday morning in 2011. He finally understood that this particular "ism" was a disease. That it would pickle the brains of sufferers and leave them unable to cope with even the most rudimentary tasks. That they would be incapacitated. That alcoholics like DJ and Kate were victims whose dependence on substances—and the stumbles that arose from this habit—did not make them any less worthy of his love.

As he sat on a folding chair in a basement room at Ad Care Hospital, munching a complimentary cookie and sipping coffee while waiting for DJ and other participants in a thirty-day in-patient recovery program to parade in single file and "graduate," Pete thought with shame of the time DJ has asked him to stop at a plaza in Sutton "so I can buy some cigarettes." DJ had said "I'll only be a minute, pop."

Pete had watched DJ walk toward the liquor store in the center of the plaza. He had taken DJ at his word, as he had so many times before, and would again and again—only to be made a fool of.

One minute passed. Two. Several.

Pete looked over his shoulder at Alexandra in the back seat and said "go check on what's taking your father so long for me, please, Alex."

He regretted the request as soon as it was uttered. Asking a teenager who was painfully aware of DJ's history to undertake a mission that was clearly one he should have shouldered himself filled him with self-loathing.

Alexandra did not move.

It was as if she hadn't heard Pete.

But he knew it was because she was afraid of what she would find.

Now Pete heard a man at the front of the room say "Hi, I'm John and I'm an alcoholic."

Pete was familiar with the expression. He had heard it at AA meetings he had attended with DJ. He was familiar too with the stories those present told and with the message "keep on coming" and the ring that was formed in unity of purpose at the close.

Now from the back of the room with DJ's mother-in-law, two of his daughters and Maddie sitting to his right and left he listened as John began to talk.

Before Pete was a man who appeared to be in his fifties or early sixties, as nonthreatening a specter in a white cotton shirt open at the neck and gray pants as an owl perched on a tree limb: a creature that blinked but otherwise did not move a muscle: minding its own business.

Pete studied John's face, which was as pale as an invalid's who has lain in bed for months, and thought he saw in the lines that creased it the residue of a tormented life.

"In just a few minutes," John said, "your son, brother, father, cousin will walk through that door and you will celebrate his 'recovery.' Before that happens you should know this…"

III

Pete had seen DJ drunk many times. He had seen what alcohol did to him. It didn't turn him belligerent as it had Pete's uncle back in West Endicott, who, inebriated, would get into fistfights at the Sportsman's Club and spend a night in the clink, drying out. More often that not, after the slurred speech and disingenuous movements manifested themselves (as for instance in trying to cut through a frozen piece of fish with a butter knife at 1:00 a.m.), DJ would simply lose consciousness. Pete had found him slumped over the steering wheel of his Chevy Blazer after he had backed into Pete and Mary Lou's flower bed. He had found him asleep in a vinyl rocking chair on the porch after all of his friends had left. He had seen him staring vacantly into space on a bench in front of Worcester City Hall as Pete, summoned to pick him up, leaned on the horn to rouse him from his slumber. He had seen him nod off in the passenger seat.

DJ was a placid drunk. This went hand-in-hand with his pacifism.

"…yes, your loved one has achieved sobriety and he should be congratulated for that," John was saying. "But understand that there may be further relapses. I have had mine. They cost me my job, my home, my marriage, my children, my health, my bank account, my friends. Everything. I have been clean for thirty years. That is no guarantee that I won't relapse again…

"…Alcohol is a central nervous system depressant. It acts on the chemical messengers to the brain—GABA, glutamate and dopamine. You may have never heard the word dopamine before (Pete was thinking, "I have not") but what alcohol does to the dopamine site in the brain's reward center is…it produces the pleasurable feelings that motivate someone to drink in the first place…"

Pete was listening intently. He had thought that John would be extolling DJ and his fellow rehabilitated addicts for their commitment to "the program." Instead here he was giving a lecture on the pervasive influence of booze on a person's mental stability. This wasn't what Pete had come for. He had wanted to see DJ walk up and "get his coin" as he had seen him do at AA meetings after six months or two years clean. Maybe hear DJ say a few words about "The Big Book" and what is principles meant to him. He was good at that.

"…if your loved one has been drinking for a long time," John continued, "he may not be able to stop, completely. The disease has that kind of hold. If he has been drinking heavily since he was fourteen or sixteen, there is a strong likelihood that he has not matured beyond that age even if he is forty or fifty now. It has robbed him of those years in between. He is caught in a time warp…"

Pat was stunned by this revelation. He sat bolt upright in his chair.

"It makes perfect sense!" he thought. "Who knew? DJ is in his late thirties but he is no more responsible in his conduct today that he was when he drank his first beer back in Vestal! This explains the misplaced keys, the lost wallet, the inability to concentrate, the compulsion to sleep late, the lack of motivation—all of it.

"What a jerk I have been not to recognize the symptoms! DJ is ill. Seriously ill!

"...when your loved one wants a drink again, and he probably will, he will spare no effort to get it. He will lie. He will cheat. He will beg, borrow or steal…

"...You must stand firm. He will fall and there is only so much you can do. He has to help himself. He won't accept the reality of his situation until he hits rock bottom. You cannot be the enabler. You have to cut him loose. It doesn't mean you don't love him. But it's the only way, otherwise you are dragged down with him…"

John finished his talk.

Afterwards, Pete hugged DJ. DJ felt whole to Pete. Healthy again. Pete could see in his blue eyes the same determination to stay the course that had been apparent when he crossed the finish line as one of the top runners in the sprint that had closed out his month at Outward Bound. Pete remembered how he and Mary Lou cheered lustily at the sight of DJ huffing toward them, rosy-cheeked and smiling. DJ perspiring, tanned, brimming with energy, exuding a newfound zest for life.

But that had been twenty-one years ago.

John was right.

DJ Nash would not be able to shed the label "alcoholic." Or the stigma that is attached to the word.

It would stick to him, like a burr, like a tick, forever.

Even if he never took another drink.

CHAPTER SEVENTEEN
THE PETE THEY KNOW AND LOVE

Pete Nash appreciated how evocative his children were in heralding his accomplishments as a newspaperman, as a prominent member of the Worcester-area business community and as a husband and father.

"How ironic," he thought. "Each is his or her own way still smarting from the ordeal I have put them through and yet all of them effusive in their happiness for my success."

Their repeated recognitions of his drive to excel and their exclamations of pride in him—"way to go, dad!"—as honors he received for his work accrued, meant more to him that the "official citation" of commendation he received from the Massachusetts State Legislature, which hung on a wall in his office. It was signed by, among others, Gov. William F. Weld.

Their accolades surpassed in worth too the plaque he was given by the Board of Directors of the Webster Square Business Association during its annual meeting at Clark University "for your exceptional leadership, your passion for Webster Square and your irreverent humor over four years as president;" than the "Action Hero" award with a framed Superman-like caricature of him that he got from the Worcester Community Action Council for the write-ups he had given the nonprofit in testament to the fuel assistance and other programs it ran for those in need; than the salutes that a city and region had bestowed upon him.

Maddie, DJ and Kate knew of their father's popularity, the prestige he had obtained, the friendships he had forged.

What they didn't know was how deeply Pete wished for them the same satisfaction in doing; and the same thrill he felt in achieving.

Maddie and Kate had joined Pete and Mary Lou at a table in the rotunda of Union Station in Worcester for an awards ceremony hosted by the Martin Luther King Jr. Business Empowerment Center, when Tim Murray, then lieutenant governor of the Commonwealth, rose from a chair on the dais, moved to the podium, scanned the faces of the more than one hundred people in the audience, and began an introduction of Pete.

Pete did not know that Murray had been chosen for this task; that he had been recruited by the organization's president, Robert Thomas, to deliver remarks that would illuminate who this workaday journalist was. He had no idea what Murray was going to say. Their paths had only crossed a few times; once, Pete recalled, while exchanging a cordial "good morning" at the Dunkin' Donuts in Kelley Square. Pete was on his way to Franklin St., Murray to Beacon Hill, where he was second in command to Deval Patrick.

Pete knew from what others had said, however, that Murray, who had served as Worcester's "boy mayor" (a moniker bestowed on him for his perpetually youthful appearance) was a regular reader of Pete's business column in the *Telegram & Gazette*.

"The Nash table" at Union Station included not only members of Pete's family, but the newspaper's publisher and his wife. A flush came to Pete's face as, caught by surprise, he listened to Murray's portrait of him in a voice that fell like a soft rain on the heads of those in attendance. Murray was talking about what a valuable commodity Pete Nash was in bringing to light in print, for the community's benefit, every week, news about the merchants and business groups whose enterprises kept the local economy humming. He was extolling Pete for the copy he wrote for full-color "neighborhood pages" that showcased commercial parts of the city—Tatnuck Square, Webster Square, Grafton Hill, Park Ave., Quinsigamond Village. These in fact had proven so popular that they now included the suburbs: Rt. 9 East, Rt. 9 West, the Blackstone Valley, South County.

Sitting there, trying not to look embarrassed, Pete was stunned by the sincerity of Tim Murray's brief speech. "There is nothing contrived about it," Pete thought. "Nothing that would suggest he is just going through the motions. He obviously feels a genuine regard for my contributions—as I do for his. I will never forget how generous he has been, toward me, tonight."

On two previous occasions Pete had been similarly championed in public, both times by his friend John J. DiPietro. Theirs was a mutual admiration society from the start. As a flamboyant, witty and savvy media personality who was frequently chosen to emcee events around the city, DiPietro quickly adopted Pete as someone who could call attention to his unscripted performances. "As if," Pete would think, "they needed a boost." DiPietro's stand-up routines were as good as any Pete had seen. His ability to keep audiences charmed, and laughing, were a constant source of amusement to Pete. Once Pete invited "Johnny D" to speak at a luncheon meeting at Livia's Dish. DiPietro had begun to render his remarks when the door to the restaurant opened, behind him. Three women entered. "Welcome, ladies, take any table, make yourselves comfortable," DiPietro said, without missing a beat. "You'd think he owned the place, or was the maître d," Pete thought. Laughter all around brought a smile to Pete's face.

Pete saw John DiPietro as a sort of lucky charm.

They had gotten to know each other during Pete's eleven years at the newspaper. When Pete wrote a book of reflections on "life, liberty and happiness" and tied each chapter's message to a Rock & Roll artist and the song he or she was famous for that fit the theme he was addressing and entitled the book *Whole Lotta Shakin'*, he asked DiPietro to say a few words about him at a launch party at Maxwell Silverman's Toolhouse. DiPietro rose to the occasion. By the time he was finished, Pete's own enthusiastic introduction of a local band, Cathy's Clown, was guaranteed to be well received.

"I stumbled across these guys playing at Leicester Town Hall one night when Mary Lou and I were returning from a fall foliage ride in Western Massachusetts," Pete said. "You will love them!"

Within minutes, almost everyone was up and dancing to rollicking Fifties music that would have made The Everly Brothers, Chuck Berry or Fats Domino proud.

John DiPietro had befriended Pete in countless ways. He invited him to dinner in the cafeteria at Assumption College, from which DiPietro had graduated and subsequently received an "Alumnus of the Year" award. He introduced Pete and Mary Lou to Kenny Rogers before a show the legendary country singer was putting on at the South Shore Music Circus in Cohasset, and encouraged Pete to give "The Gambler" a sign copy of *Whole Lotta Shakin'*.

In May of 2006, DiPietro gave Pete a copy of his own book *You Don't Have To Be Perfect To Be Great/Lessons From Superstars On How To Build The Life Of Your Dreams*. It was inscribed "To Pete Nash—the man that is everywhere. I am amazed you get to so many functions!"

DiPietro saw Pete Nash as "a player."

That it hadn't always been that way, that he had been required to pull it together, and quickly, for the benefit of Mary Lou and the children, after "the debacle of Brookline," made Pete's subsequent triumphs that much sweeter.

II

He was keenly conscious of how Mary Lou, Maddie, DJ and Kate had chosen different ways to demonstrate their pride in him.

Twice in 2005 Pete was touched by gestures he did not see coming, first from Kate and then from Maddie.

Pete and Mary Lou had picked a warm day in October to visit Old Sturbridge Village. Mary Lou had been there before, as a child, on a Jenkins family trip. Pete had attended events in the Oliver Wight Tavern at OSV and checked out the gift shop but never been through the grounds. He was enjoying "New England's largest outdoor living history museum"—the curated lawn, the costumed characters and the trade shops—when his cell phone rang.

It was Maddie, designated dialer for Kate.

"Dad, Claude's having car trouble, can you come?"

"Where are you?" Pete asked.

"The Webster House. We're here for dinner. I didn't know who else to call."

Pete hung up. "Again!" he said. "Again, our plans are interrupted by our children needing something! We'll have to head back to Worcester." He could not help but think of the times he and Mary Lou had returned to Vestal for visits with family only to have to pick up and leave upon hearing of a crisis involving DJ or Kate.

His mood, until then ebullient, turned sour.

The sight of Chris Liazos standing in the middle of the restaurant's parking lot when they arrived seemed odd to Pete. Stranger still, Chris taking time from his many responsibilities as owner of the place to personally direct Pete toward one of the few open spots left on a busy Saturday early evening.

Chris and Helena Liazos's restaurant was a favorite. They had met and begun their romance at the Webster House and then put their mark on the menu. The atmosphere was something worth every bit of the positive notice they received from an admiring and worshipful public.

Over the years, Pete would be a frequent presence at the Webster House, for business lunches, for wine dinners, for New Year's Eve out with he and Mary Lou's friends Harry and Linda Berkowitz. The friendship that developed between Pete and Chris would last beyond the closure of the restaurant and Helena's death.

Chris led Pete and Mary Lou inside, past the bar, up the stairs to the function room. Pete had been in the room many times. He had taken time to check out the photos of famous personalities that adorned the walls.

Tables in the room had been arranged in a U-shape to accommodate a crowd of about sixty people. Looking around, seeing so many familiar faces, Pete was flabbergasted. "Almost the whole side of my family from New York State! Bill Thayer my high school pal from Springfield! T&G colleagues! Mary Lou's sister Sarah and brother-in-law Joe from Vestal! All of our grandchildren! What a turnout. What the hell!"

The shout of "surprise!" was followed by a rendition of "Happy Birthday." Looking around the room, seeing a cross section of the people who made up his life, Pete was humbled.

"You knew, didn't you?" Pete said, turning to Mary Lou, and then to Chris Liazos.

Kate Nash had worked with her brother and sister for weeks, making the arrangements. She had used the telephone and email like a telemarketer to gather commitments. She had told prospective attendees to keep the event a secret. She had put together an "everything-Pete" poster board that stood at the entrance to the room.

Pete accepted the microphone that Chris Liazos handed to him, identified each person present by name and thanked them all "for sharing my 60th with me."

Chris drifted away, as the platitudes began. Mary Lou, Maddie, DJ, Kate and Pete and Mary Lou's eldest grandchildren spoke.

Kate, referencing Pete's love of boxing, said, "pop has achieved a lot but I don't think he is ever going to be the middleweight champion!"

Reporting for work on Monday, Pete was greeted by Moe Guarini, who ran the T&G's "Newspaper in Education" program. Moe was a veteran of the industry and a sometime college professor who had taken Pete under his wing and encouraged the connections Pete was making with the business community.

"That's the best party I've ever been to!" Moe said.

III

Two months later, on Christmas morning, Maddie presented Pete with a scrapbook. Gazing at its soft, light brown cloth cover, which was embellished with faint swirls, like a schoolgirl, doodling, would make, feeling the heft of it, leafing through its pages, he knew it was one of the finest gifts he had ever received. He knew too that as a scrapbooking enthusiast, Maddie had poured hours of labor into creating the scrapbook. She wanted her efforts to reflect those he had exerted in writing a memoir of his youth in the Village of Endicott.

"I will cherish this always," Pete told her. "I will never let this out of my sight."

Sometime soon after the publication of his book, as the purchase orders came flooding in from across the country—from people who had grown up in the village or whose family members had, from those whose relatives had worked for the shoe company or the big manufacturer of business machines—Pete turned a boxful of cards and letters of congratulations and newspaper clippings over to Maddie.

"See what you can do with this, please, Maddie dear," he said.

Knowing how much gratification her father had gotten from the book's widespread approval, Maddie had squirreled herself away for days and weeks on end, sifting through what she had to work with, and organizing it.

The result, Pete thought, as he sat in a chair with the scrapbook in his lap later that day, was a masterpiece. Maddie had sprinkled the pages with words of inspiration: "CREATE." "BELIEVE." "DREAM." She had created a pocket for a note of congratulations from "Coach Angeline," around whom the book was written, and the coach's son Chris. She had included an email from Pete's colleague Dick Broszeit that began, "Pete, guess what. Sold your book on eBay. That didn't take long, did it?" There was a clipping from the Binghamton newspaper, announcing that Pete would be making an author appearance in his hometown; correspondence from the Barnes & Noble in Vestal: "we would be happy to carry the book in our store;" a letter from John Dellos the quarterback: "Pete, I can't wait to read your book. Someone who lives in California told me about it."

In the back of the scrapbook Maddie had posted a letter to Pete from the director of the visitor center in Endicott. Blood rushed to Pete's cheeks as he read it again. He remembered himself in the visitor center's community room the previous November, facing a crowd of well-wishers, talking about the book, seeing Coach Angeline make a late entrance, pointing the coach out.

Dear Pete,

Your book is enriching us! The book has been flying off our shelves...in fact we are down to one copy. Could you please send more? We will be happy to pay for shipping.

I hope you will consider another book signing, perhaps in the spring when the weather is more predictable. I believe there is so much interest in the book and you have captured the spirit of the village so well, that it will continue to resonate within our community.

Kathy Utter
Endicott Visitor Center

By 2019, the volume of memorabilia associated with Pete's career filled several banker's boxes. None of it meant more to Pete than the scrapbook Maddie had done for him.

"Someday," Pete said to Mary Lou, "I am going to donate all my papers to a library, for public perusal, like a president or a noted author would."

"No one's going to be interested in that stuff!" Mary Lou said.

She didn't even look up from the afghan she was crocheting.

IV

DJ's way of honoring his father was to cultivate and shape Pete and Mary Lou's yard, on a corner lot. He did this by planting rhododendrons and clematises and hydrangeas and roses and lilacs, by pruning, by fertilizing, by mulching, by undertaking cleanups in the spring and fall, by transforming a small property from a barren landscape into beds of seasonal color that even butterflies and hummingbirds found to be a pleasurable refuge from the hustle and bustle of the state highway—a block away.

Pete was more than glad to leave this to DJ. Over the years, employed by various landscaping companies, DJ's knowledge of grasses and flowers and shrubs and trees had increased tenfold. He was for all intents and purposes a horticulturalist whose expertise Pete found to be invaluable. He was also not averse to the kind of grunt work that would have quickly sapped the staying power of many a seemingly more robust landscaper.

Pete appreciated too that DJ had survived nearly slipping into a coma after being stung repeatedly by hornets at a job site. An epi pen administered by paramedics had probably saved his life. He had brushed against a bush and stirred up a nest and been swarmed. Even someone as big and strong as DJ would have been helpless against such an onslaught, Pete thought.

Pete hated to think how close to death DJ might have come, that day.

He often smiled in thinking about how DJ tried to show him the right way to "broadcast" mulch; or just in contemplating DJ's irritation with him when he didn't use a rake or a shovel in the most effective manner.

He loved telling people, "my son's a landscaper."

With exuberant pronouncements of his love with text messages and poetry, DJ lauded Pete as the man he most admired. Burdened as he was by the conviction that Pete had caused the family irreparable harm by forcing it out of its cocoon, distraught as he was by Pete's sometimes apparent indifference to the problems that had arisen from The Move, DJ still understood, unequivocally, that Pete had gone above and beyond for the four of them.

DJ's many eruptions, his repeated contentions that Pete bore responsibility for the pain and suffering that consumed him...despite these...he knew there was another side to the story.

One year, in a "Happy Father's Day" rhyme to "The Man, my pops," DJ penned these lines and presented them to Pete in a gold frame:

He rushes around to grab the best story

84

To deliver his readers that article with great glory
So recognized for his achievements while always in a hurry
Awards given proudly hang on his wall, one from Lt. Gov. Murray
All my life I've seen the man so passionately fight
To chase his beloved career, provide, live in love, do what's right
So many accomplishments dominated with greatest grace
Always easily overcoming trials, tribulations, dilemmas he'll face
Words really can't describe how proud he does make
The most loyal, kind, caring, generous, devoted guy, never fake
My life without him I can't even imagine or think
That instantly brings me to an overwhelming sobbing brink
He gracefully and most thoughtfully ran to be there
For myself, his family, friends, work and whoever he does care
Hr Hr Hr after hr, family first while typing articles for 50+ years
Him showing me strengths, hope and believes to be a man overcome my fears
I could carry this poem on all about him forever
Because he's my idol, my maker, my friend, father I treasure
He's never had a ticket, broke the law or become a villain
By far #1 super fan of his, only idol the legendary Bob Dylan
Him truly going above and beyond definitely living a balanced, peaceful life positively
Carrying all the weight, following through, conquering life definitely
For ten straight years, overseeing visits with my darling kids
One amazing family feat, not blinking an eye, he's did
Finally left to say, dear Dad, on Father's Day
To have you, watch you, put all effort into all you can
Why I write this poem for you The Best, The Amazing, The Man!

DJ would admit to Pete that his rhymes were simplistic. As were Horace Nash's before him, the ones DJ's grandfather had written to his beloved Beatrice—from whom DJ had drawn inspiration to compose his own. He nevertheless wrote hundreds of them, filling notebook after notebook, asking Pete to type some of them up and print them out for him ("on better stationary, dad, the good stuff") so that they could be framed and given to one of his daughters, one of his sisters, his manager at the supermarket where DJ was bagging groceries—when the supervisor's mother died—or in remembrance of his rooming house buddy Rick from the North Shore.

Few in the family thought much of DJ's poems. This bothered Pete. He knew how hard DJ had worked on them, deep into the wee hours of the morning, sometimes. DJ would read them aloud. The response would be tepid at best. Then he would put them back into a file folder and probably, Pete thought, try to shrug off the sense of rejection that was overwhelming him.

Only Pete and Maddie showed the slightest excitement.

Pete encouraged DJ to dip into the work of Tennyson, Keats, Shelley, Robert Burns, Frost, Emily Dickinson and Whitman for guidance and a determination toward improving his technique. Pete almost handed him a paperback collection of William Wordsworth's poems that he owned but then decided against it.

Pete's previous attempts to share with DJ poetry of a high caliber had always been met by the observation "I like mine better."

So it was left as another tie that bound Pete and DJ, father and son, like their discussions of music and sports, and this was enough for both of them.

By emulating a hobby his grandfather had pursued, DJ was holding onto the threads Horace Nash had left behind. He was doing his best to perpetuate a side of Grampa Nash's personality that he respected and indeed revered—just as Kate held on to Gram Nash's wristwatch come hell or high water.

As for Pete, by lifting up DJ's poems as deserving of praise (even if, Pete thought, they weren't necessarily good enough to be shared at poetry readings around Worcester County that DJ kept saying he wanted to attend), he was continuing his efforts to make amends for past slights.

Besides, Pete thought, it made no difference if DJ's poems were sophomoric or that they might never win a prize.

It was the work that went into them that mattered.

IV

With few exceptions, Mary Lou had cooked dinner for Pete for all the days of their lives. She marveled in reaction to him always, without fail, thanking her, afterwards, as they cleared the table and he began washing the dishes which was his part of the bargain. It was a routine they had long since settled into, a distribution of duties that seemed equitable on the face of it but Pete knew otherwise. Mary Lou deserved most of the credit. Even though she took for granted that setting out mac-and-cheese (the best he had ever tasted, crusty delicious on top), corned beef and cabbage, a roast from the crock pot, kielbasa with oven-baked potatoes, chicken scampi, chicken parmesan or angel hair pasta with meat sauce were her God-given responsibility, he knew that she was bringing more to the relationship than he was. While he often kidded her, "I got you for the two dollars I paid for a marriage license at Vestal Town Hall, what a steal," he knew in his heart that she would have been worth a million times that amount. Her preparation of meals, virtually seven days a week, night after night, year after year, hardly ever asking "can we get Chinese from King Jade?" or "I'm in the mood for a pan pizza with black olives and sausage from Domino's," was not a contribution he had even considered her making when they began dating. His only infatuation then was her body—and the lust that drove him to the edge of distraction, awake or asleep, until he could have her again.

Pete was pretty sure that no one, not Maddie, not DJ, not Kate, grasped, completely, the depth of his love for the woman who had stood by him through the dark times. He was certain that Mary Lou had not confided to them what she had revealed to him, recently, during one of those candid exchanges between them that popped up so unexpectedly but also so regularly. It had been so long in coming that he was shocked to hear it, despite all of a negative nature that had transpired.

They were in the car, making their Tuesday run to the supermarket, Pete at the wheel. Mary Lou, as a concession to her bad knees, had given up driving. They were talking about "what was" and "what might have been." Rehashing, as they had on many occasions, how things had gone wrong. Not just at the outset of their life in Massachusetts but now more than thirty years later. Maddie and Claude's marriage in shambles. DJ and Kate still in the grip of addiction in their mid-forties—he on meds for depression and occasionally alcohol, she on booze. Pete had known for a while of Mary Lou's profound disillusionment, her discouragement with their circumstances and with the toll aging was taking on her body that often prompted her to say to him "I don't like being me;" the annoyances with his pursuits that troubled her but that she had, like the stalwart she was, buried, in the interest of maintaining.

He did not know, however, how close she had come to packing it in.

"There were times," Mary Lou said, "leaving the rest home, getting on 290, when I said to myself 'instead of taking the exit for 146 I could take the one for the Mass Pike. I could be back in Vestal in a few hours and put all of this behind me."

Pete said nothing. He nodded. He knew by this admission that only Mary Lou's belief in them had kept her from such a drastic recourse.

V

As with any marriage that withstands setbacks and attains permanence, Pete and Mary Lou's in the 52nd year of their union had suffered its portion of nicks and scrapes.

"I am sure that Mary Lou has her disappointments and regrets, as I do," Pete often thought.

At seventy-three, pushing seventy-four, and holding onto better health than Mary Lou, he was in no mood to slow down. Accustomed as he was to being active physically and socially, he bristled at the notion that her movements were restricted; that a cane or crutch were now necessary for her to get up and down stairs; that her zest for going—to the Outer Cape, to quaint seaside towns on the North Shore like Newburyport and Rockport (which she loved as much as he did), to an outdoor concert at Indian Ranch at the edge of Webster Lake, even to a movie, a wedding or to Virginia Beach to see their friend Gretchen—had been supplanted by a desire to stay put.

As fans of the TV show "Wahlburgers," they had talked of visiting the family's original hamburger joint, in Hingham. Of going back to Patriot Place in Foxborough, which they hadn't seen since Robert Kraft's vision of a destination complex as an addendum to Gillette Stadium had begun to come together. Of satisfying Pete's yearning for a look at Mark Twain's home in Hartford. Of a weekend at the Irish Village in South Yarmouth—an affordable getaway and one they had made a number of times.

None of this was happening anymore.

Resentment festered in Pete as he deliberated how to get Mary Lou interested in dinner in the North End of Boston or on Federal Hill in Providence; or in taking a drive to the Brookline Booksmith near where he used to work so that he could secure a copy of Toni Morrison's *Beloved*. "The Big E," Massachusetts' state fair, the world-famous flea markets in Brimfield, fall-foliage rides into the Berkshires with a stop for lunch in Northampton: all scrubbed from the calendar like a teacher erasing scribblings from a chalkboard.

"That part of our life is over," Pete thought. "What I would give to have it back! Gone! But we can't hit the rewind button, like Mary Lou does on the remote when we want to see a scene from a show we've recorded again, or check on the identify of a character whose name we can't remember.

"There is no going back."

VI

Fresh in Pete's mind was a fall Mary Lou had taken the previous September, and his expanded role as part-time caregiver that resulted from it.

On a Saturday, Pete had taken "The Boy," as Maddie called Mitchell, to the record store in downtown Worcester. Pete hadn't intended to be away for long.

He knew Mitchell would like "Joe's Albums." Pete had been in the place, had perused its hundreds of vinyl issues, covered in plastic sleeves and neatly arranged by artist and genre in bins along the walls of the store. Pete was always on the prowl for used records, just as he was for previously-read books. His collection of LPs had grown over the years, although still meager compared to that of his friend Harry Berkowitz's. Still, whenever Pete had the chance and a little money in his pocket, he would head to the flea market in Douglas or Grafton, or to a garage or yard sale where he knew there were records available. In this way he had gotten his hands on Paul Anka and Johnny Rivers and Joan Baez and so many of the musicians he derived enjoyment from.

Pete and Mitchell were in the store a while, sampling and sorting. Pete picked up four or five albums, put several back—holding onto a Johnny Cash and relinquishing a Neil Young, picking and choosing, staying within budget.

He let Mitchell browse to his heart's content.

About forty-five minutes passed.

Exiting onto Main St., walking past the doors to Mechanics Hall, mentioning to Mitchell "we saw Ronan Tynan, the Irish tenor, here recently, with Uncle Joe and Aunt Sarah," he then acted on a hunch.

"I never have enough time to spend with my grandson," he thought.

"Would you like some lunch? Pete asked. "Have you ever heard of Coney Island, the hot dog place on Southbridge St.? It's famous."

They ordered chili dogs, chips and sodas at the counter. Mitchell seemed impressed with the line cued up for purchases even before they gravitated to an empty booth with their order. Pete figured Mitchell understood without being further enlightened that the restaurant was a local institution, a no-frills kind of spot save for the big neon sign out front; that the well-to-do and the not-so-deep-pocketed alike often chose it as a place to eat—and to be seen.

Mitchell immediately began reading the names and messages that had been carved into the ancient wood paneling, as he soaked up the history of one of the city's landmarks.

"This place is cool," he said.

At home in Northbridge, shortly after Pete had left, after drinking a cup of coffee and having some breakfast and still in her nightgown, Mary Lou descended the two short flights of stairs to the bathroom. She would brush her teeth, make the bed, change into her clothes for the day.

She was used to Pete's absences, his life on the go. She was used to making the best of it; of seldom complaining about whether he was gone for an hour or half the day. She always welcomed him back with a heartfelt "hi, babe, how'd it go?" Only rarely would she say "I thought you had deserted me," or "what took you so long?"

Mary Lou was almost finished in the bathroom when the cold-water faucet handle sprung loose as she turned it off. "God, no!" she said aloud. Water gushed as if from a geyser, splattering her, soaking the floor. With her typical Jenkins calm when faced with a problem, she managed to open the door of the cabinet beneath the sink, reach in and close the valve.

As she did, she lost her footing. She lurched and fell heavily to the floor.

Mary Lou lay there, unable to get up, with her head resting against the toilet, for the next two hours.

When Pete put the key into the lock to open the front door, he heard Mary Lou's shouts of distress.

"PETER! Down here! Help!"

Pete tried to lift her.

"Call an ambulance," she said. "I hope I didn't break any bones!"

Three Northbridge EMTs listened to Mary Lou explain what had happened, Pete looking on despondently, guiltily. She was breathing heavily.

Together, the EMTs helped her into a sitting position and then got her to her feet.

"I'm okay, I guess," Mary Lou said.

Listening again to Mary Lou describe her mishap after the EMTs had left, Pete thought "this is us, now.

"What a creep I am for again putting my interests first.

"Above hers."

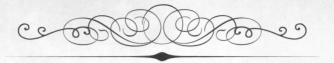

CHAPTER EIGHTEEN
A RECKONING

One morning in August of 2019, Pete was sharing with Andrew Bates an abbreviated version of "the story of us," particularly as it related to the plight of DJ and Kate.

He had met Bates only an hour earlier, upon arriving at a just-opened detox facility in downtown Millbury, outside Worcester, to garner information for an article he would write about the place.

Pete and Andy Bates had clicked the instant they shook hands at the entrance to the building, which was from the rear.

"A friend of mine was a founder of this event," Pete said, showing Bates a brochure for "Sober in the Sun" that he had picked up on his way in. The thirty-first annual edition of the Labor Day weekend experience—which featured live music, camping, recovery meetings, swimming and canoeing, health rehabilitation workshops, dances and so on— was coming up at the Treasure Valley Scout Reservation in Rutland.

The site was rustic and secluded. Joe Cutroni Jr. would be ensconced in a tent in the woods for all four days, this year. Pete had joined him there on the expanse of grass at the bottom of a long hill a few times to listen to the bands.

"Is he still sober?" Bates asked.

Pete was caught off guard by the question. He laughed. "No, Joe and I have a beer here and there," he said. "Mostly when we're going to see The Green Sisters at Stone Cow Brewery in Barre or The Mavericks at Indian Ranch in Webster."

Defensively, Pete added, "but neither of us is a raging alcoholic. We just enjoy a brew, out, now and again. Sometimes at Foxwoods, or at Mohegan Sun before a concert. Joe was in radio, ran a small station near Clark University in Worcester. He knows many of the folk and rock musicians I like. We have a lot in common. Our mutual love is music."

Bates was a burly man with a pleasant personality, eyes that Pete could tell were filled with compassion for those who struggle, and white hair. He smiled while leading Pete down a hallway into the nerve center of the facility and said "I've been in the recovery business for twenty-three years and I've only helped one person stop drinking. Myself."

Pete knew exactly what Bates meant. Alcoholics are never "cured." It's a lifetime disease. Pete thought of DJ, dependent for years on Suboxone; of reading, in Jennifer Weiner's *All Fall Down*, about how the medication "blocks your receptors, so you can't take the heroin, or the Vicodin, or the Oxycontin." How it stifles your urge for whatever narcotic is tempting you. How it gives you some opiate but not enough to get high, just enough so you feel okay.

II

They were sitting in Andy Bates' small office with cups of Starbucks coffee from the cafeteria after the tour of the facility Pete had been given. Pete liked that Bates chose to sit in one of the two armchairs in the room, rather than behind his desk. It put them on an equal footing.

"I'm writing a book," Bates confided to him.

"What's it about?" Pete asked.

"My life trying to help people in their recovery from addiction. I call it 'Recovery with Dignity.' It's a series of vignettes. I've been working on it for seven years!"

"Stick with it!" Pete said. "Don't give up on it!"

Pete decided to share with Andy Bates what came next.

"I have almost finished a book that recounts our travails after I moved the family to Worcester in 1985, the tremendous remorse I feel for the difficulties my wife and children have faced. I'm calling it *For Pete's Sake*. I picked that title as a play on my single-minded pursuit of my goals at the expense of their welfare."

Pete went on to explain how he had spent all of the time since trying to deliver compensation by being a dutiful steward of the family's interests. How even today he was still putting himself out there for DJ and Kate as chauffeur, money lender, morale supporter and so on—often over Mary Lou's objections.

"There is no way I can tell everything, reveal all of the sordid details," Pete thought.

"It would take weeks."

Bates listened, nodding his head, digesting what Pete said.

"It sounds to me as if you have more than made up for any grievances they may be holding onto," Bates said.

"Don't beat yourself up about it anymore. You have no reason to blame yourself any longer."

Driving back to Northbridge, Pete thought about what Bates had said.

"He's absolutely right," he thought. "I can be at peace with it."

He wondered, however, if Mary Lou, Maddie, DJ and Kate could ever completely feel the same way.

CHAPTER NINETEEN
'YOU HAVE TO COME HOME, NOW'

Daily, usually even more often than that, Pete would undertake an accounting of where their lives stood. He was prompted by some force deep within him to initiate this tabulation, just as he was compelled to spend several minutes reflecting on the pages of *Sophie's Choice* or *The Naked and The Dead* he had read the day before—prior to picking up the story again.

This practice had become ingrained in him and so was part of his routine, as normal an occurrence as shaving, balancing his checkbook—or setting his alarm clock, although he knew he would probably wake up at 6:00 a.m. whether it buzzed and flashed on his nightstand or not.

These were personal, private ruminations. He didn't want to saddle Mary Lou with them. She had enough to worry about without hearing from him the current "grade" he was assigning their circumstances. Besides, it would remain a D minus as it had for so long. She didn't need an explanation from Pete as to why this was the case.

Asked by his brother Myles how his book was coming along at the wedding of Myles's son James in Waterloo, New York in June of 2019, Pete said from across a linen-covered table in the ballroom of the lakeside hotel where the reception was being held "fine, the only thing I'm not sure of is whether it's going to be a happy or a sad ending."

He did kind of suspect, however, that it might conclude badly.

DJ and Kate were no closer to conquering their addictions.

II

Pete was at a sidewalk sale in neighboring Uxbridge on a Saturday earlier that month, snapping pictures of clothing hung on racks at the curb, a hot dog vendor in a Koopman Lumber shirt, two emissaries of a state representative hawking popcorn, a couple dressed as clowns. He was absorbed in the festive atmosphere under sunny skies. He had stopped at a new store with a window overlooking a bubbling tributary that ran from Capron Falls and was chatting with the owner of the shop—a gallery. She had quickly made it a haven for local artists and their work.

Within about thirty minutes Pete had gathered enough material for the article he would write for the next issue of the weekly newspaper he was freelancing for in semiretirement.

His cell phone rang.

"You have to come home, **now**," Mary Lou said. Pete recognized the unequivocal firmness contained in his wife's tone; that there would be no point in even saying "why, what's wrong" or "I'll be there soon, I'm almost finished here."

"She's on the back porch, drunk as a skunk. I locked the door. I won't let her in the house. But you have to come. Now."

Kate was on the porch swing.

"You can't do this," she said.

She reeked of alcohol. Pete thought of all the times she had ridden next to him in the car, that stale scent he so hated, the one that reminded him of the bars his uncle used to frequent—when he walked past them. So familiar, so abhorrent. He thought of the strength of Kate's beauty, the lushness of her hair and skin, when she was sober, and the weakness of her will when she was under the influence, intermingled, like a film of oil in a bucket of water.

"I live here," Kate said.

"No, you don't," Pete said. "We've been letting you stay here since you started getting weekend passes from Rhodes House, remember? I take you back every Sunday night. You live *there*."

"I'll call the police.

"I'm going to have Mary Lou arrested. She tried to kill me. Choke me. That's the second time."

"Do I never learn my lesson?" Pete thought. "Do I ever let DJ and Kate stop playing me?"

"When will I stand my ground, not let them have their way?"

III

For eight straight years, up until shortly after he retired from the *Telegram & Gazette* in 2013, Pete had made arrangements to rent a two-story beach house at the terminus of a dead-end street at Hampton Beach, two blocks from the ocean, on the bay side, from a co-worker and friend. Pete and Mary Lou's grandchildren had practically grown up there, one week each July or August. Incredible memories had been created. The grandkids talked about "our Hampton summers" incessantly, long after the transaction ended with Marty Pratte's decision to put the property up for sale.

Years passed. Maddie vowed to reinstitute "a family tradition," and she did. In January of 2020, searching the Internet, she found a small rental on Manchester St., off Ashworth, in the same general vicinity as Marty Pratte's place. She booked it, with Alexandra's help.

"We're going to Hampton again, and we're going every year from now on!" Maddie announced.

Once, on Johnson Ave., as night fell, with everyone congregated on the deck and a brilliant orange-red sunset glowing behind the now-shuttered Seabrook nuclear power plant, Mary Lou and Kate had gotten into an argument. Pete couldn't remember what it was about, only that Kate and her then-boyfriend had been drinking all afternoon up the street at the home of someone they had struck up an acquaintance with.

Things had quickly escalated.

"You and Stanley have to go," Pete said. "Pack up and leave."

When Kate refused, Mary Lou grabbed her by the shoulders and tried to move her toward the stairs from the deck to the driveway.

Mary Lou's hands slipped.

"Did you see that? She's chocking me!" Kate screamed.

Now here was Kate making the same accusation.

"It's not true," Mary Lou had said before Pete went out to confront Kate. "I didn't lay a finger on her. I just told her she couldn't come back into the house. Ever! I locked the door!"

There was between Mary Lou and Kate a history that contributed to a gulf, growing ever wider, that Pete realized might never again be bridged. There was the issue of Mary Lou's missing wedding ring, despite her diligence in hiding it where she thought it couldn't be found. Kate had to be the culprit, Mary Lou insisted. She had opportunity. Kate denied it. When Mary Lou announced that it was gone, Pete checked at several pawn shops in Worcester. "File a report with the police and we'll go from there," he was told. "Bring us a picture."

"What's the point?" Mary Lou said. "She hawked it. I won't be getting it back."

There was too the most recent altercation before this one, Pete and Mary Lou ushering a wobbly Kate to the front door, Kate resisting, Kate swinging her purse, whacking Mary Lou in the face; as if to say, "take that, I'll fix you for being such a mean mother." Pete spared the humiliation, Pete left to again berate himself for always coming off as the good guy.

"Tell you what," Pete said to Kate. "*I'll* call the cops. I'll save you the trouble."

Pete led the officer who responded through the house, explaining as they went what was going on.

The uniform and the reasoned voice must have worked its magic. The officer talked Kate out of her threat to have Mary Lou arrested for assault and battery. He coaxed her down the side stairs and into the street.

Pete watched as Kate started to walk away. "Why do I feel so forlorn, when all I see from her is aggression and defiance?" he thought. "I should be incensed at her behavior and I am but I also feel dejected at the hopelessness of the situation."

"She can't get away with this!" Kate shouted. "I'll press charges. They can't make me leave! All of my belongings are upstairs!"

"This is Kate the alcoholic talking, not the Kate who when she's around and not drinking is so easy to live with, to laugh and joke with, who empties the dishwasher for her mother without being asked, who cleans the tub, who makes dinner to give Mary Lou a break, who calls Mary Lou and I her best friends."

"Kate, move along," the officer said. "If you don't want to do that, you can spend the night in lock-up."

"How quickly it unraveled," Pete thought. "She had it all together. All those weeks working herself back to sobriety, working with Mass Hire and Mass Rehab, being outfitted with stylish new designer clothes by the folks at Dress for Success, the photo I took of her looking sharp in black before reporting for a job at Arcade Snacks in Auburn, the definition of regained health that I posted on Facebook—publicizing her resurgence. Gone!

"That intelligence, on a par with that of a student who is always on the honor roll! That personality, luminous enough to light up a room with no electricity! That promise, flush as a full house at the poker table! That investment I've made, trying to help her regain her footing!

"All wasted!

"How my heart aches," Pete thought. "The daughter I prize so dearly, who repeatedly succumbs to the lure of alcohol, who inches so close to a complete turnaround only to fall back into her old destructive ways."

Kate was walking slowly toward her friend Edwin's house a block away, knowing that he would take her in. Even with two children and his mother living under his roof, Edwin, a black tech-company worker, would make a place for her. "This is part of the problem," Pete thought. "Just as I let her walk all over me, so do the men in her life come to her rescue. She has her network. She uses Facebook to maintain contact with any number of them and they are there for her when she is facing homelessness. It is never the right guy, though; it is always someone who will tolerate her habit, in exchange for what? That is not so hard to figure out."

Pete and Edwin texted back and forth and after three days Kate agreed to check herself into Spectrum. Pete knew the place, a complex of buildings situated on scenic grounds off Rt. 9 in Westborough. DJ and Kate had both detoxed there before.

"At last," Pete said to Mary Lou, "we will be empty nesters for good. No more letting DJ or Kate come back. No more caving in."

"Pop," Kate said, when she telephoned several days later, "can you bring me some sweatpants and sweatshirts? It's cold here. A pack of Maverick 100's too. Please?"

Pete was used to responding to these sugary-sweet requests from her. The idea of her sober was enough to kick his willingness to be of assistance into high gear.

He was fishing through thirty-three gallon black plastic bags in her old bedroom, thinking about the labor he had put into repainting and redecorating the room to make it into guest quarters, just as he had turned DJ's old bedroom, next to Kate's, into a home office.

"I can assure Mary Lou at last that neither of them will be living here again," Pete told himself. "It shouldn't have taken me this long. I'm done with it, so help me God."

Pete set to work pulling pieces of Kate's wardrobe from a bag and tossed them onto the futon she had been sleeping on. Jeans. Socks. A long-sleeved New England Patriots shirt.

Reaching deeper, he felt something solid.

He yanked the top of the bag open wider.

His hand latched onto a plastic bottle.

"Of course," he thought. "She's been drinking Barefoot Pinot Grigio. She's probably been drinking all this time she's been bunking here weekends. Right under my nose. And look at all of them. Dozens more!"

Pete read the label on the bottle he had removed from the bag.

"Get Barefoot and have a great time!" it said.

His hand grasped hold of a Fireball, Cinnamon Whisky; "Red Hot."

"That's what they call Kate at the places she's been," he said. "They call her Fireball."

Turning the bottle around, he saw the message printed on the label on the back.

"Ignite the night."

CHAPTER TWENTY

DJ'S TORTUROUS TRAIL

In conversation and by text DJ often used the expression "I can't catch a break" to remind Pete of the setbacks he had been dealt; and was still facing every day.

It took years for Pete to amend his usual reply of "so sorry, you deserve better" and substitute "be grateful for what you have," or, "you know, DJ, this problem was of your own making."

Pete would concoct preposterous schemes that he thought might save DJ from himself. One of these involved taking charge of his son's movements, from dawn to dusk; charting and shepherding his every step, as he would the pieces on a chessboard, so as to ensure that he knew where he was and what he was doing—all the time.

The idea came from a book Pete had passed along to DJ: *The Journeys of Socrates*, written by Dan Millman: an odyssey of "courage, faith and love." DJ loved the story of the orphaned child (Sergei Ivanov, or Socrates) in Tsarist Russia who grows up in a land of smoldering discontent and is forced to flee an elite military academy. Socrates escapes into the wilderness, with nothing to cling to but the memory of his grandfather and the promise of a gift buried near St. Petersburg.

DJ identified with the tale, as Socrates encounters mentors, masters and a mortal enemy.

"This is my plan," Pete dreamed. "I will take DJ with me to the newspaper office on Franklin St. in the morning. He will be dressed as if for a long hike. He will have no money, just a peanut butter and jelly sandwich and an apple. I will assign him a route to walk. Send him up Pleasant St., perhaps, into the west side of the city. Or down Southbridge St. to Cambridge St. and then a right on Main St. which will take him past Clark University on his way back. He will have a notebook and a pen in which to record his observations about what he sees and feels, the people he encounters, the neighborhoods. He will stop long enough at the entrance to Clark to write down his impressions of the statue of Robert Goddard.

"When he returns, he will head to the library a block away on Salem St., read the morning newspaper, maybe pick up a biography of Abraham Lincoln—or Bruce Springsteen or Jim Morrison or Ted Williams which would probably be more to his liking.

"With not a dime in his pocket, with limited opportunity to obtain alcohol, with only a schedule organized to the minute and a regimented routine in front of him, DJ will put his time to productive use and my mind will be at ease. I will be able to define his actions, like a puppeteer who guides the motions of a wooden doll with strings or wires."

Pete was at his desk, ruminating on the plot, which had kept him awake half the night, when he suddenly realized how crazy it was.

"Who am I kidding?" he thought. "It is not only farfetched, DJ would find a way around doing my bidding."

II

The forces that had conspired to undo any likelihood of success—the ones imposed on DJ by outside influences, and those that were self-inflicted—were painfully obvious.

There were the OUI's, now stacked so high that DJ probably would not be able to drive again; to reacquire the license that had been snatched from him by the Commonwealth eight years ago. These were not even worth talking about, they had both decided. DJ was too far in arrears on child support. He would have to square things with the Massachusetts Department of Revenue before he could even bother walking into the Registry and applying for reinstatement.

A state ID—for bank transactions, food stamps, prescriptions—was doable. But when DJ's expired in January of 2019, in attempting to renew it, he hit a snag. His original birth certificate, from Johnson City, was frayed and rumpled almost behind recognition..

"This is no good," a female Registry worker, relishing the authority she wielded over a customer who she apparently saw as fair game for rejection, told him.

DJ put the twenty-five dollars back in his wallet.

"Story of my life," he said, as he and Pete left.

Pete sent away for a replacement. Now DJ had the three forms of ID that were required.

The months ticked by. Pete once and DJ the next time would say "we have to get this done."

Nearly a year passed before they did.

III

DJ had been living in the rooming house in Oxford for three years when he rekindled a relationship with Jennifer Younce. Looking at her from across the room at the PIP shelter in Worcester, long before this, he had thought "that girl is gorgeous." Now, half a dozen years later, with DJ downstairs and Jennifer up, they began getting reacquainted.

DJ quickly tagged her with the nickname "Gemifer—because she is so sweet and priceless, dad." Pete would think how good DJ was at coming up with nifty identifications for people and places he admired or despised; he had dubbed the Section 8 complex in which he and Kylie and the girls lived—Orchard Hill—as "Orchard Hell." Thinking recently of the band of misfits with whom he co-resided, he said "I call this not a House of Cards but the House of Nuts."

Pete had been saying to him "you should find a nice Methodist girl. It's time." He had warned him about hooking up with anyone who carried the kind of baggage that would jeopardize his recovery.

On visits, while she was waiting for DJ to shower or otherwise get ready, Jennifer would hold Pete captive with talk of her mother who had died in a car crash when Jennifer was young, her father in Texas who she seldom saw or heard from, her sons, her lack of self-esteem, her failure to win favor.

On and on she rambled from her spot on the sofa opposite Pete in the parlor.

Pete saw across from him a woman about DJ's age, whose freckled face had probably once been pretty but was now filled with anxiety. She was short and small with tiny hands, long reddish-brown hair and a figure that he could see had been compromised by the weight she had put on.

Most of what she said to him made no sense, it was delivered in such a torrent of gibberish.

"She's a basket case," he thought.

"This environment is a breeding ground for misery," Pete had told DJ. "You don't want to go down that road again.

"Remember Harmony?"

DJ's tumultuous affair with Harmony Rodriguez lasted only a brief while. They were both on the street when it sparked. They started to run together and in no time at all they were occupying a first-floor apartment on Siegel St., off Millbury St., in the southeast part of the city. From the mattress they had thrown on the floor, which served as their bed and living room couch in one, they would hurl shoes at mice scurrying along the baseboard while cursing the Worcester city councilor whose family owned the building, for her neglect of the premises.

Pete did what he could to help them. They fended as best they could. They walked to the St. John's food pantry on Temple St. mornings, for a free breakfast served by Billy Riley. They hung out with all sort of beggars, tramps and thieves on the Worcester Common. They headed to the Salvation Army on Main St. for lunch or to Everyday Miracles on Pleasant St. for a meeting and then it was back to Siegel St. where their deplorable living conditions and lack of sustenance fanned the flames of discord.

Pete knew that DJ knew Harmony was no bargain. Semi-homeless, she had been with various men, white and black, crack heads and four-time losers. She was suffering from Crone's disease. Pete wondered what other diseases she might be carrying.

One morning, in the midst of a raging argument, Harmony called the Worcester PD and had DJ arrested for domestic assault.

She didn't follow through. She didn't bother showing up in court.

Her absence might have been all that saved him.

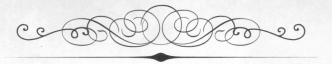

CHAPTER TWENTY-ONE
AN EXCHANGE OF LETTERS

In the twilight of his life, as he felt the weight of the years on his shoulders, Pete Nash spent an inordinate amount of time mulling what was, what is, what might have been and what will be.

He recalled reading in William Styron's book *Sophie's Choice* a sentiment expressed by "Stingo" that looking back serves no useful purpose. Still he could not resist the urge, in taking stock, to ponder at length the Nash family's past, present and future.

His destiny, his blessed course, had been set almost from birth. He recalled the different vocations he had been enthralled with as a boy, when gripped by an early yearning for a livelihood. Cop, firefighter, superhero, gas-station owner, ballplayer, teacher, soldier, preacher: all of these prospective careers drifted across his consciousness at various times, like deer crossing a road. Or the sheep his mother told him to count when he was having trouble going to sleep.

What stuck was an earnestness to put words on paper. To write. He seemed to understand, instinctively, that there would be a satisfaction—rewards—that went far beyond any income he would receive for his efforts in that vein. He seemed to grasp that writing would open doors for him. He must even then have realized that through these portals would come people with whom he would strike up friendships that lasted for many years.

Initially, in the 1960's, there were the games he was assigned to cover in the Sports departments to which he was connected. In Binghamton, in Plattsburgh, in Newburgh. After that came the short stories he began to create as a way to veer away from the fact delivered in reportorial fashion to the fiction that would allow his mind to run free. He fell under the spell of authors he read and wanted to emulate: Dickens, Twain, Faulkner, Henry James, Steinbeck, Dreiser, Eudora Welty, Hemingway. They were the models from whom he would draw inspiration for his own ambitions. He devoured their works, searching for the key in their craftsmanship that would unlock his own powers of composition. Inevitably there would be books penned by his own hand. He knew none of these would rise to the caliber of *The Old Man and the Sea*, *Crime and Punishment* or *The Adventures of Huckleberry Finn*. But this did not stop him.

After mostly retiring from newspaper work, Pete spent the first several hours of the day hunkered over his laptop, in the solitude of his office on the second floor, a three-dollar scented candle from Walmart burning on his desk, as he tried to kick-start a masterpiece. He did this, as Stephen King had recommended, in the best tutorial on writing that Pete had ever read, without fail. Let nothing get in the way of this commitment, King had said. It is essential to picking up the thread, maintaining continuity, realizing what you have set out to do.

Pete followed Stephen King's advice to write seven days a week without exception. On Easter morning, on Thanksgiving morning, on Christmas morning. He was always up early enough to do so. He told himself "it doesn't matter if I never gain the credit I am looking for. There will be the delight of having made something from nothing; of adhering, too, to a quest for individual fulfillment:, of reaching for the proverbial unreachable star."

Pete wished nothing less for Maddie, DJ and Kate. It had become more apparent to him by the day, however, that maybe only Madeleine Anne would shake herself loose from the restraints that had held the three of them back. In middle age, she had pushed the ugliness of the years immediately following the family's move to Massachusetts aside and replaced it with activities that gave her life meaning. Mothering. Keeping a house that demonstrated her pride in home ownership. Scrapbooking. Creating colorful seasonal wreaths from items she purchased at the dollar store where she worked. Turning away from the substances that had caused her such grief and embracing health instead.

II

Pete wept when he came across a letter Maddie had written to him in January of 1988. He had been rummaging through boxes of stuff he had held onto with the idea that one day he would organize it in a way that his children, grandchildren and great grandkids would appreciate: postcards; letters; photographs; office memos; thank you emails for the boost he'd given a startup business, a community initiative or a charitable cause. There were even handwritten notes from first-grade classmates of Cassandra's at the Rice Square School in Worcester as a testament to an appearance he had made. Whenever he spoke to students, Pete would tell them they should consider journalism as a profession; that they should not rule out the Fourth Estate as a means of making a living before fixing on medical or financial or law or education.

"You might not get rich," he would tell them, "but you will never lack for excitement. You will never sit around, bored. You will get free passes to all sort of special events. You will meet some of the most interesting people in the world."

Maddie's letter was written on two sheets of notebook paper in her familiar careful cursive, the words faded, barely recognizable they were so faint, the paper itself dotted with rust spots. Pete was standing next to the large six-drawer oak desk he had purchased for fifty dollars from a former co-worker when she was downsizing to a smaller place. He had had to remove the thick top, which was fastened underneath with wood screws, and the drawers, to get it into the house and up the stairs.

He was surprised to find the letter after all this time. Thirty-one years! Maddie had written it so long ago that he had to think about the circumstances she described. In rereading it now, he could see that she was under duress at the time, and trying as best she could to understand what she had done to justify the rejection coming from himself and Mary Lou.

"She was so young!" he thought. "Not yet eighteen! How could I have been so blind to the alienation she was feeling?"

Only a little over two years from her attempt to flee Worcester and Massachusetts, Maddie was on her own. Tensions between Maddie and her mother had prompted Mary Lou to throw her out.

Tears ran down Pete's cheeks, as he read her words.

Dad,

I know you must be very disappointed in me! I'm sorry for whatever I did to make mom not want me. I need to make you guys proud of me by trying to do good in school, which I was, and by staying out of trouble, which I was, and by keeping a job, which I have. But you always seem to find fault in everything I do. I don't care anymore whether you believe me or not. But I don't do drugs, and drink, and I've never lied to you about that and I've never drove and drank.

I'm sorry if you think I'm a bad influence on DJ and Kate. I don't think I am. I feel sorry for mom, she's so naïve, she doesn't even know what goes on with DJ and Kate. She's gonna find out someday and it's gonna hit her hard. She has never found weed on me yet she caught DJ with it more than once and believed it when he said it wasn't his! Ya right! That's funny!

Dad, I'm not a bad person. I hope you know that. You have always been my favorite person in the whole world. I love you with all my heart. Because you've always listened when I talked, you don't jump to any conclusions, and you understand things. You taught me that too.

Pete paused, walked into the upstairs bathroom, took a tissue and wiped his eyes. He sat in his swivel chair, at the desk, and read on.

Whether you know it or not, I'm more responsible than I used to be, I think. I know you think I'm stupid for not going to school. But I have a job interview tomorrow (Friday) for a secretarial position and if I don't get it I'll go back to school on Monday. I wanna graduate. But right now I need money. I know you say I'm welcome home anytime but I could never live with mom again. I can't get along with her, although I love her a lot. She'll always be my mom. I said some things I'm sorry I did, so I'm sorry, mom. I hope you forgive me. I miss DJ and Kate and I miss you most of all, dad. I hope your new job is going well and I hope you're happy.

There's also I wanna say, I'm sorry you don't like Jamie. I love him with all my heart. I can't leave him cause I can't be without him. He may not be your first choice for me. But I love him. Maybe you can try to understand how I feel. Anyways I'm doing good. I've been getting up early and watchin' Becky for Mrs. Smith while she's at school and I've worked every night. I'm workin' Saturday 4-11 cause we're doing inventory and Sunday 8-12 for inventory. So that will give me more hours and I worked four nights this week. That's pretty good.

Jamie got a full-time job working 6-2 for $7 an hour. So he's doing good. We're busy. I'm helping Mrs. Smith a lot cause she's studying a lot.

Dad, I hope you don't hate me and I hope you'll always wanna see me wherever I am. I miss you an awful lot. Please don't stop loving me. I hope someday you forgive me for whatever I did. I'll try hard to make you proud of me even though I'm not with you every day and even though I can't talk to you every day. I've always reminded myself about everything you told me about getting an education.

Please tell DJ and Kate I said hi, and mom.

I guess I'll go to bed now cause I worked today and I get up at 6:30. So I'm tired.

I love you with all my heart and miss you, dad. You're the best father in the world.

I'll love you always,

Maddie

Pete turned the pages of the letter over. On the back of the second page Maddie had written, in parentheses, "Pops only."

His body shaking with regret, he laid the letter aside. He stared at it, digesting, over and over, the message Maddie had conveyed. Wondering if he had really ever understood what hurts he had inflicted by forcing the family to buy into his lofty ideas for personal growth.

"I have prospered but oh how they have suffered," he thought.

"Did I reply to Maddie, then?" he thought. "I must have. But I'm not sure."

Opening his laptop, Pete pecked out the following, in Microsoft Word.

Dear Madeleine Anne,

In going through my vast "archives," in trying to toss some of the material and hold onto only the most significant, which you or others in the family might want to examine (and which can then be burned in the fire pit in your backyard), I came upon a letter you wrote to me many years ago.

A response, if I did not issue one at the time, is overdue, given all that we have been through.

You start your letter by saying "I know you must be very disappointed in me." You were living on your own, with Jamie. You were honest in revealing your situation and your feelings.

In rereading the letter now, I am filled with remorse for my actions.

I am painfully aware that I put you, DJ, Kate and mom in a precarious position by moving us to Massachusetts. You make clear, in heartfelt terms, that you were a good person with an eye toward making something of yourself despite the disadvantages I placed on you. A strange city, a strange neighborhood, a strange school.

How overwhelmed you must have felt!

You have done what you said you would. You could have succumbed to the pressures I placed on you. Instead you have persevered. You are the world's best daughter, sister, wife, mother, aunt, niece, cousin and friend. No one can have a greater legacy than that.

No one but you knows how much you have overcome to become the woman you are today at the age of forty-eight. As a father, I beam with pride whenever I say your name or see your face.

You would have every reason to still resent me for what I did, jeopardizing rather than safeguarding the futures of my children and my wife. But you don't. We are all aware that you are far too noble a person to hold grudges or to retaliate out of spite. For that I am grateful.

In the book I am writing about our ordeal, I hope to explain some of the factors that motivated me to take the job in Brookline. They are more complicated than you might imagine. But they are no excuse for not thinking things through better so that at least I could have given all of you a fighting chance to make the adjustment without the difficulties that arose because of the move. I cannot say with certainty that "our story" will ever find its way to a publisher. Even whether it will be presented as fiction or nonfiction. Only that I want to tell it. I want to draw a sympathetic portrait of all of the principals—except maybe myself! My hope is that it will resonate as a story of a family that is carried forward by a love for one another that defies all roadblocks and tragedies; and that it will be a story with a happy ending.

Disappointed in you? I could never be. The girl who at fifteen, who as a sophomore in high school, was forced into such a drastic recourse, has come through. Done so, in fact, in more ways than you may give yourself credit for. Whatever disappointments you feel about the course our lives, and yours, have taken, please know that I know only joy in being the father of a daughter who is the same gentle and giving and gracious soul in 2018 as she was in her tumultuous teen years.

I shudder to think how differently things could have gone for you. How you could have been swallowed by a city that claims its share of victims. How you might never have met Claude or experienced the thrill of giving birth to Casssandra, Jocelyn and Mitchell. How you might have ended up as an article on the front page of the newspaper after being kidnapped—or worse.

I cannot change the decision I made or what transpired as a result of it. I can only hope that by sharing our story I am able to bring some perspective to it.

I needed to say this much, if nothing more gets said—or written.

I needed you to know I love you, Maddie. Who you are and what you mean to me. I needed you to know that your letter of three decades ago is proof that you were determined to demonstrate to me that you were not a disappointment.

How wrong I would have been to ever think you would be.

Your goodness shines through every moment of every day.

DAD

CHAPTER TWENTY-TWO
I'M SO LONESOME
I COULD CRY

Pete was tuned to WUMB, as usual, while driving to and from the corner for the newspaper the morning of September 17, 2019. It was just before eight o'clock when he swung into a space next to the shopping cart rack in the plaza's parking lot and got out of the car.

"Butch" and "Buzzy" were already at the door of the Dollar Tree, the first of six to ten people who would get in line to buy the newspaper for a buck—or a third of its regular price. John, aka "Cuckoo;" "Pablo;" "Steve;" "Dick."

"Francis," the town's only conspicuous homeless man, was propped against a wall a few feet away from them. He was smoking a cigarette, his mangy bedroll and crooked walking stick lying beside him. He was a portrait in brown from the thick straggly hair on his hatless head to the battered shoes on his feet. He had become a source of amazement to locals for having lived out of doors for going on two years. No one could say for sure where he rested his bones at night, only that he would reappear shortly after dawn, trudging north or south on Providence Road, slump shouldered, lost in thought. Sometimes jabbering to himself. Sometimes making small circles with his hands while standing in front of Dunkin' Donuts or Speedway, as if preaching to a hastily convened congregation.

They could talk about Francis in muffled tones, which they did. He would pay them no mind. In the same way, he brushed off offers of help that had been extended to him by cops and concerned citizens.

"Leave me alone," he would say.

Whenever Pete saw Francis, he thought of DJ. He remembered a time when he went to pick his son up from the PIP shelter in Worcester, for a medical appointment. He could tell that DJ, in his revulsion for the place, had chosen to sleep in the woods overnight rather than be subjected to the indignity of its austere and dungeon-like confines.

DJ smelled of campfire. Pete pictured him clustered with other woe-be-gone drifters around a dilapidated steel barrel, trying to stay warm.

Pete had said nothing as DJ slid into the seat next to him and helped himself to a stick of gum from the pack of Trident that his father kept in the cup holder of the car. It would refresh his breath, just as, Pete knew, it would mask the odor of alcohol that was so often on the tip of his tongue.

II

Returning with the Tuesday edition of the newspaper, Pete heard mention of Hank Williams as WUMB's "Artist of the Week," in honor of the 96th anniversary of his birth, and then Williams's distinctive high-pitched voice—clear and resonant as a siren's in the still of the night—singing "I'm So Lonesome I Could Cry."

"Quite the coincidence, WUMB celebrating Hank Williams as the Ken Burns 'Country Music' special airs on PBS," Pete thought. "I should call Harry Berkowitz, who has long been a devotee of Hank Williams, and tell him. Harry will want to check out the show if he hasn't done so already."

Pete could feel an ache sweep over him as he listened to the second stanza of the song:

Did you ever see a robin weep
When leaves begin to die?
Like me, he's lost the will to live
I'm so lonesome I could cry

"Hank Williams, dead at twenty-nine, DJ struggling to stay alive at forty-five," Pete thought. "DJ I know is consumed by the same kind of loneliness that Hank Williams felt, and sang about. Autumn is at our doorstep, the leaves from the towering oak out back—the one DJ has trimmed for me to keep its lower branches from interfering with the lawn and the flower bed—will start to wither. Winter will follow. Winter, the hardest part of the year for him. Christmas, the holiday, the carols, he has come to hate; not because he doesn't love Jesus. No...it's....I am not sure what. Maybe it's because he remembers Christmases back in Vestal, at our home, at Gram Jenkins's home, and has experienced nothing so special. Maybe just because it is one of those holidays, like Thanksgiving, like New Year's, when he is most apt to drink again. That and the darkness of the season, which worsens his already despairing mood.

"I know how much DJ yearns for the companionship of a woman. He has been without one, for the most part, since Kylie ordered him to leave all those years ago—on Father's Day. He blames himself for that relationship ending even though there was never a chance it was going to work. They were incompatible from the start. He drank and she slept around."

Pete recalled DJ alluding to him recently how much he would welcome a female in his life. Pete had been telling him he should make connections at the supermarket and he had agreed. "I know, you're right, pops, a lot of pretty women come through the checkout line. When I'm bagging I'll say to most everyone 'have a nice day' but when an attractive woman shows up I'll say 'come back. PLEASE!'"

"He misses Jennifer, who moved out of the rooming house several weeks ago. Her departure has left him rudderless.

"Worse," Pete thought, "is his detachment from his girls. Especially Amory, who he is closest to. They have shared so many happy moments, shooting hoops, walking the paths and skipping stones at Buffumville Dam, exploring Purgatory Chasm, playing cards, watching movies, eating a dinner he cooked for them, shopping at the mall, texting back and forth.

"His girls are older now. Amory will turn eighteen in April. That would explain why they have less time for him. But I know, and DJ knows, it's the drinking. They cannot stand the thought of him hurting them again. It always costs him more when this happens than it would someone else, because of his history. It has ruined many occasions."

Pete recalled how DJ's girls had turned on him in the summer after discovering that he was drinking at Tyler's fourth birthday party. Pete and Mary Lou had left early, their energy sapped by the heat. Pete learned later that DJ kept disappearing, walking to and from Maddie's car to sip on booze he had stashed in his backpack.

"They recognize the symptoms. We all do," Pete thought. "When he gets sloshed he gets more boisterous, more eager to tell his war stories. They laugh at them but then they realize he is under the influence and they pull away.

"It takes him forever to earn another shot. Even then, he never gets a complete pardon."

III

By his own admission, DJ had flirted with the idea of suicide three times. The only instance Pete had direct knowledge of occurred during a snowstorm in February of 2015.

DJ had taken a job at the small neighborhood convenience store a block from Pete and Mary Lou's home. Pete was already cashiering there. The store's owner liked DJ. "When he came in for a candy bar or a soda when those kids were growing up, he was the most polite," she told Pete.

When June Leonard and her husband moved to Florida, Brenda Morrison told Pete she would hire DJ. "I know I'm taking a chance on him," she said. "This may be just what he needs to get his life together."

He struggled to learn which buttons to use when ringing up the sale of a gallon of milk, a loaf of bread, an Italian grinder, a jar of tomato sauce, a pack of cigarettes, a can of soup. Mastering a separate machine that was utilized for the sale of Keno and Lottery tickets gave him fits.

"Don't worry," Pete said. "You'll get it. It took me a while."

DJ enjoyed commiserating with the customers. Pete had told him this was the best part of the job, getting to know the regulars and exchanging pleasantries with them. Many of them, Pete said, "will tell you their life story. You never know what you are going to hear!"

DJ and Brenda clicked. They would smoke together on the bricked patio in front of the store, DJ confiding to her his hope of starting his own landscaping business, Brenda telling him about her favorite vacation spot—Aruba—and her favorite car: the Lexus.

"Customers say to me 'how can the owner of a little store like this afford such a fancy car?' It's like they resent my success. My daddy taught me how to manage money. I lease the car, pay it off ahead of time and get into another one. It's the one luxury I allow myself. That and Aruba."

Brenda in her jeans, short-sleeved top and sneakers and with no lipstick and her bleached blond hair dropping straight to her shoulders listened to DJ vent—as he often did with Pete.

She consoled him. She brightened his mood.

"He has a lot of anger," she told Pete. "He needs to get rid of that or he will never be happy."

"He holds me responsible for the direction his life has taken," Pete said. "I'm hoping, waiting for him to get past it."

IV

With each DJ falter, there were repercussions. This is something Pete had tried to emphasize to him, that there is a ripple effect, that he is not the only one who suffers the consequences.

He had been living with Pete and Mary Lou again, and drifting into a pattern of showing up for work late.

"Brenda won't stand for it," Pete said. "She is counting on you."

On a Friday, DJ left the house at two o'clock to take over for Brenda.

"Where is he? He didn't come in," she said, when Pete answered her telephone call.

He looked at his watch. 3:30 p.m.

"I'll be right down," Pete said.

Pete kept calling DJ's cell phone, to no avail.

The snow began falling just as dusk settled in, palm-sized flakes blowing in from Providence Road so that Pete had to go out every half hour or so and clear the patio and walkway from the parking lot.

Finally DJ answered.

He recognized the irritation in Pete's voice. But invariably, at times like these, he turned any criticism back on his father.

"You don't understand," he said. He was crying. "No one does. I try but nothing goes right."

"What are you talking about?" Pete said. "Where are you?"

"Walking up Hartford Ave.

"A snow plow is coming down the hill. I'm going to stand in front of it."

V

DJ texted Pete just past ten o'clock one night in September of 2019.

"Are you in bed asleep yet?" he asked.

"No," Pete replied.

"I'm sorry dad but I need a ride to the ER. My back and stomach are killing me. It's those two kidney stones and the cyst they said I had the last time I was in. Ugh!"

Before dropping DJ at the curb next to the entrance to the ER at St. V's and parking the car, Pete said "have you been drinking?"

"No," DJ said.

Pete knew otherwise.

Watching DJ through the windows as he walked toward the ER, Pete could see that he was impatient. He shuffled in place. He looked lost. Not a friend in the world.

Pete had brought Alice Sebold's *The Lovely Bones* with him. He took a chair and began reading, keeping one eye on DJ as a nurse asked him questions and took his blood pressure.

The next time Pete looked up, DJ was gone.

After an hour Pete inquired about him and was led into the ER and down a corridor on one side of which were nurses and doctors, standing, talking, working at computers. Having come from a nearly empty waiting room, Pete was stunned to see how many people were congregated in the area set aside for them, as he was by beds lining both sides of the narrow passageway. Patients bandaged, patients half asleep, patients muttering to themselves.

He turned a corner as told to and there was DJ.

He seemed more content than Pete had expected him to be. Pete realized it was because, in crisis, he was being tended to. He was safe.

They talked briefly.

"You don't have to stay," DJ said. "It will be a while. Go home to ma. I'll text you when I'm ready."

Pete said goodbye.

"If I don't respond when you text, keep trying," he said.

Departing, Pete heard DJ say to the woman lying in a bed in front of him "there goes pops."

"My boy," Pete whispered to himself. "My precious son. God don't let me lose him."

VI

Back from the hospital, DJ confided to his father that "they did nothing for me. No one but you and Maddie and Amory care about 'ol DJ."

Pete refrained from saying "it's because you came in inebriated. You were not a high priority. If you had showed up sober, in excruciating pain from the kidney stones, they would have been more attentive. You were just another of dozens of discards in those corridors who by inflicting harm on themselves lost any chance of gaining sympathy. Patients with legitimate reasons to be there would be treated first and with TLC. Can't you see that?"

Several days passed.

Pete didn't hear from DJ.

"I don't know if he's alive or dead," he said to Mary Lou. "I know he hasn't gone to work. That's always a bad sign."

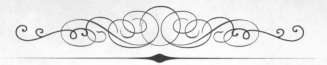

CHAPTER TWENTY-THREE
WELCOME TO WOOSTAH!

It might have been because he had grown up experiencing the family unit as an indestructible institution that Pete Nash had such a hard time accepting anything less than this for his own extension of it.

It was hard for him to believe that it could be fractured, broken beyond repair, lying on the ground in pieces like Humpty Dumpty. That not even an Albert Jenkins the Fixer, the Grandmothers Grace and Beatrice, Jeanne Nguyen the Counselor or Barry Judd the Preacher could pick up the shattered bits and meld them back together—whole as they were before they were laid to waste by The Move.

Born in 1970, Maddie had been spared the turbulent Sixties: the assassinations, the rise of the counterculture, the civil rights marches, the protests, the riots and the Cuban Missile Crisis. The Vietnam War too in all of its tragic futility, its tremendous loss of life. Several of Pete's high school classmates would die in Southeast Asia before Maddie started kindergarten at Clayton Avenue. She, and DJ and Kate after her, would spend their formative years cradled not in the maelstrom that was the decade preceding theirs but in the comforting lap of Big Bird, Bert and Ernie, Fred Rogers, The Waltons, Captain Kangaroo, the Vestal United Methodist Church and the living rooms and backyards of their grandparents' homes—where no harm could come to them or their cousins.

It was their Age of Innocence, just as the Fifties had been Pete and Mary Lou's. Pete's own youth might have been even more idyllic and made even more secure than his children's by the stabilizing influences of Ozzie and Harriet, Sky King, Roy Rogers and Dale Evans, Superman, Mickey Mouse, Lassie, Rin Tin Tin, the George F. Johnson Public Library, the Enjoie Park pool, the Endicott Boys Club, Beach's Bicycle Shop, Mr. Ed and the Saturday-afternoon Game of the Week with Dizzy Dean and Pee Wee Reese at the microphone.

There was not much by way of unsettling in Pete's world, at West Corners Elementary in the early 1950's, save for an occasional air-raid siren and talk of bomb shelters.

The expectation, for Pete and Mary Lou, in starting a family, was more of the same for their children. There was no reason to think that a continuation of "Happy Days" was not in the offing. There would be Legos and Barbie dolls, Tinker toys, pot-roast suppers, ice cream, the corner candy store, Sunday school, Gram Nash's themed cakes when birthdays came around, barbecues in Joe and Sarah Sweeney's driveway and watermelon seed-spitting contests at Lucas and Sally Rae Olsen's home on Katherine Lane (how Pete delighted in DJ retelling the story of older cousin Toby Olsen's anger when DJ outdistanced him in this competition).

In surrendering to his urge for something more, Pete in 1985 had turned his family's perfect tableau upside down. His children's world had started out like the nontoxic one he and sister-in-law Sally Rae had entered in the maternity ward of Ideal Hospital forty years earlier, ten days apart (the standing joke in the family was that Pete and Sally Rae had slept together long before Mary Lou came into Pete's life).

Pete had yanked Maddie at 15, DJ at 11 and Kate at 10 from the house Grampa Nash had built for them, from the neighborhood peopled by the Thomases and the Pierces and the Klingensmith's and the O'Brien's and from a town that exuded nothing but graciousness and deposited them in a city seemingly seething with alienation toward outsiders.

"Welcome to Woostah!"

II

The Move had eventually worked for Pete Nash. That it hadn't, so much, for Mary Lou, Maddie, DJ and Kate pricked at his conscience. It laid there, a painful reminder of how he had let them down.

Now in her seventies, and unable to walk far without the aid of a cane or a crutch—or Pete's arm—Mary Lou's contentment came in large measure from enjoying the company of her grandchildren and great grandkids. Oh, she and Pete were alright. Whatever bitterness she had once harbored toward her husband for his shortsightedness now lay beneath the hugs and kisses and displays of affection and bursts of camaraderie that carried them through the seasons.

Theirs was a life and a routine rotating around coffee together in the morning, trips to the supermarket or Walmart or BJ's, lunch and dinner, TV time in the evening and an ever-present discussion of books they were reading or had finished. Their tastes in this regard ran in different directions for the most part but their affinity for the written word did not and so the books piled up. In refusing to part with any of the titles he had acquired including first editions, hard-to-find hardcovers and works by celebrated novelists Pete's collection grew and grew—like Jack's beanstalk.

"You have a lot of books!" Kate's Evelyn said one day in going into the bedroom she used to occupy, where Pete had stacked hundreds of books.

Mary Lou's solace came from this and from working the Wonder Word puzzle in the newspaper, finishing another row of an afghan, conversing long distance with Sarah, experimenting with recipes she saw on "The Pioneer Woman," Ina Garten's show or as these were presented by the folks from The Kitchen. She watched documentaries about animal life (she and Pete had both been captivated by the camera work involved with "Serengeti") and how-to programs. She shopped at Kohl's. She joined Pete for dinner out.

It wasn't enough, not nearly what either of them had thought their life would come to with less money, less travel and less fun...but it had to suffice.

III

Approaching fifty in 2019, Maddie had shed many of her insecurities, become a strong woman and solidified her position as a bedrock of the family. Pete could see in her devotion to her parents, her brother and sister, her children and her nieces and nephews a willingness to be the one they could lean on. Her desire to bring everyone together for birthday celebrations, cookouts, Easter-egg hunts, group chats, pumpkin carving, Thanksgiving at her table and Christmas morning at Nana and Pop's was more well-received even than the chocolate desserts she came armed with—most Saturdays. Her consideration for others knew no limits. Her radiance seemed to grow by the hour. Her commitment to shedding pounds (despite Claude's grumbles that she lived on "three bananas a day") stood as testament to her faith in a brighter tomorrow.

Maddie. The girl who had run was staying put and making the most of it.

DJ at forty-five remained plagued by difficulties that were as onerous as they were incomprehensible—to Pete. DJ's increasingly frequent bouts with poor health went hand-in-hand with a certainty that he would never get ahead. It was almost as if his troubled past had coalesced into a hopeless present, no matter how much exertion he put into trying to carve out a life for himself.

DJ vacillated between high and low. His stabilizer switch, like the one on Pete's Canon, was Amory Beatrice. She always eliminated the blur, brought everything into clearer focus for him. The youngest of Pete and Mary Lou's grandchildren, she was seventeen now, leggy and gorgeous, exuding a quiet calm, utterly devoted to her father, assuring him that no matter what nothing could come between them. Theirs was an alliance that Pete was counting on to see DJ through the crises that would surely continue to materialize.

Donald Jeremiah Nash. Racing against time to find peace and happiness.

Kate at forty-four was on her third stab at recovery.

"She always thrives in a structured environment, like the rehab house she's living in right now," Pete thought. "Fits right in. Ms. Personality. Keeps the other women loose. It's on the outside where she has a hard time coping. Hooks up with the wrong guy, drifts back into the old habits. Can't resist picking up."

Katherine Rose Nash. An angel in the morning when sober. A devil of a handful when drunk.

VI

Pete was reading Terry Daugherty's biography of Joan Didion—*The Last Love Song*—in the fall of 2019 when he came across a comment Didion's husband John Gregory Dunne made to their young daughter Quintana after her cousin Dominque had been found strangled in the driveway of her home in California.

In an attempt to counter Quintana's feeling that the school Dominque was attending, or "the curse of the suburbia house," was responsible for Dominque's death, Dunne told her "it all evens out in the end."

Joan Didion, Daugherty says, assumed that Daugherty meant that "good news eventually balances the bad."

Quintana, however, interpreted her father's remark to mean that she shouldn't be surprised, "that sooner or later, everyone *else* will get bad news, too."

The idea that the good and bad in life are intermingled and that the positive will ultimately be counterbalanced by the negative, or perhaps vice versa, so that when all is said and done the weight is distributed in equal proportion, as on a teeter totter, made some sense to Pete.

But he knew this wasn't true at all. He was aware of too many instances in which life had proven to be unfair: babies drowned in bathtubs or hurled from the roofs of buildings; families killed in horrific car crashes through no fault of their own; nuns slaughtered; young girls raped and mutilated; hundreds of innocent villagers wiped out in a hail of bullets; six Worcester firefighters lost in a warehouse inferno caused by two homeless people; the body of a small child found along the highway, stuffed into a suitcase; kids gone in an instant—their skeleton discovered years later.

Taking this into account and even with Maddie losing her husband to illness and facing the prospect of going on without him, Pete could only hope that the worst of the Nash-family ordeal was behind them.

He wished he could be sure.

CHAPTER TWENTY-FOUR
A HARROWING RETURN TO 'NEWSPAPER DAYS'

Dreams of what H.L. Mencken referred to as "Newspaper Days," in a book about the Baltimore he illuminated with such style and verve, filled Pete's nights.

They were not for Pete, however, comfortable ones, as they had been for Mencken. They should have been. Especially the last eleven years of Pete's full-time journalistic career, until he retired in 2009, were more rewarding than he ever could have imagined. It was during this time that all of his sacrifice in obligation to the work he so loved came together.

Walking into the back entrance to the *Telegram & Gazette* building for one of the first times, in 1998, falling into step with Bruce Bennett, he was surprised to see that the then-publisher knew who he was. Extending a handshake without breaking stride, Bennett said "they tell me you are going to be an asset to us."

This unexpected gesture of acceptance had a lot to do with smoothing the way for Pete. He had been hired by the advertising director, Bob Recore, not to sell ads but to write copy for business pages that would pay homage to the merchants' community in the city. Recore's idea proved to be a stroke of genius, and a godsend to Pete. Pete became the advertising department's go-to guy for coverage of sectors of the local economy that seldom attracted regular reporters' attention. Nevertheless, Pete immediately ran into pushback from the paper's managing editor, Harry Whitin, for his audacity in presenting himself as one of a circle of correspondents who, following Whitin's lead, zealously guarded their domain.

Ever the savvy and battle-tested warrior, Bob Recore succeeded in deflecting most of Harry Whitin's objections to Pete stepping on the Editorial Department's toes. As Recore and Special Pages & Sections Director Jay Valencourt saw what Pete could accomplish by illuminating with prose and pictures business areas of the city, functions hosted by the Chamber of Commerce, groundbreakings, grand openings and all kinds of goings-on involving commerce, they loaded more and more assignments on his plate. Pete didn't mind. One project led to another. Soon he was attending breakfasts and luncheon meetings and receiving invitations to various functions. Before long too his role in stroking the egos of prospective advertisers became so crucial to the performance of the department that new uses of his time and talent were conceptualized. Pete found himself out and about from mid-morning until late afternoon. He learned his way around the neighborhoods of the city. He became a regular at confabs of business organizations. He was enlisted as a board member with several of these groups. When Bob Recore and Jay Valencourt decided that editorial supported by advertising as a revenue generator in the city had the potential to produce the same results in the suburbs—in Rt. 9 East, in Rt. 9 West, in the Blackstone Valley, in North County, along the Johnny Appleseed Trail—they unleashed Pete. Full-color "double-truck" weekly pages targeting a particular region of the county followed, engendering enthusiastic praise from business people, who gobbled up advertising space, which did not come cheap. Meanwhile, Harry Whitin fumed.

"How dare this guy steal our thunder?" Whitin seemed to be asking. Pete heard secondhand that Whitin was making frequent visits to Recore's office to register complaints.

"Let me worry about Harry," Bob Recore told Pete.

In no time at all Pete was seen as one of the Advertising Department's golden boys. Ad reps flocked to his desk, asking for special treatment in print for a loyal client, or for a business that had previously considered the pages of the T&G as "too pricey" but was now enticed to think about buying space.

Pete was free to range far and wide and to bask in the glow of newfound status.

He was rewarded with stellar reviews and frequent raises.

He had never had it so good.

II

Now, however, the farther he got from that life, the more tormented he was by an entirely different, uglier vision of his newspaper days on Franklin St.

In one of these, Pete was approaching the locked glass door at the rear of the building, as he did every morning. No one used the front entrance. This would have been too much of an imposition, in that it was a whole block away from the parking lot.

Only when Pete had forgotten his lanyard with his ID badge dangling from it, which he needed to scan his way in, did he walk around and use the main access across from Worcester City Hall, knowing that one of the security guards—Rome or Walt—would recognize him and wave him through.

The dream he was having ten years removed from his T&G days flashed at him night after night. He had always been a dreamer, in more ways than one. Those he could remember in the morning, he would share with Mary Lou and she would shake her head in acknowledgement of their absurdity.

Pete was helpless to explain where they were coming from, but there they were. He would be following his usual routine, leaving the house around eight o'clock, heading north on Rt. 146, stopping at the drive-thru at Dunkin' Donuts in Kelley Square for his coffee, parking, walking toward the building with his T&G satchel with his laptop in it slung over his shoulder, his trusty Blackberry cell phone in the pocket of his sports coat, Pete already smiling at the thought of the camaraderie that existed in what had become known as "the Pete Pod." Theirs—his, Sheila, Denise, Veronica, Jack, Brooke, Ann and Marty's paneled-off area just inside the back door—was a loose-knit unit, rectangular in shape, where the close proximity of one to another resulted in an almost-constant banter. Every hour or so Stu Herman who had worked in the mailroom in the basement since high school—as quirky but loveable a "pest" as ever lived—would drop by and inspire a new round of animated chatter.

"What changed?" Pete would think, rolling and tossing, drenched in perspiration, as images of a building, and a staff, decimated, flooded his brain.

Pete envisioned himself picking through the rubble of a bombed-out structure, looking in vain for Recore and Valencourt or any of "my people," searching without success for the steps to the Composing Room.

He would wake briefly with a shudder and then recall a more positive scenario, in which, coming back from the road, he would tell Veronica Wells, with a note of triumph in his voice, "I believe I've gone and sold three or four ads for our guys, just by interviewing business people they asked me to visit."

"Pete, what did you promise them?" Veronica, an eyebrow raised in mock consternation, asked.

"Whatever it took," Pete said.

"Peter Nash!" she would reply, shaking a forefinger at him.

Pete tried to draw significance from the dream. It contrasted so sharply from what he had actually experienced. He had been "a name" around the city and the county, known to all of the major players in business, government, education, the arts. He had even written a weekly column, "Biz Buzz," with his byline and photo attached to it—unheard of on advertising pages.

What a ride it had been.

Now only a scarred version of that life was left.

"I can't figure it out," he said to Mary Lou.

"It must stand for the demise of newspapers in this day and age," she said.

Pete, however, had come up with a different interpretation.

"Maybe, just maybe," he thought, "it symbolizes all that has gone wrong for the Nash family; and my role as perpetrator of our difficulties."

CHAPTER TWENTY-FIVE
THE OLD MAN

At a gathering of the family in Northbridge for his seventy-fourth birthday on the third weekend of October, 2019, Pete's granddaughters Alise and Amory presented him with a cake, covered in plastic and streaked with ribbons of blue and yellow and green and orange. It was heavy-laden with frosting.

Inscribed on top in brilliant red were the words "Happy Birthday Old Man." These were accompanied by cards from Maddie (along with a six-pack of Sam Adams and a ten-dollar gift card to Dollar Tree) and DJ (with a poem inside), to go with ones he had received by mail from out of state and expressions of congratulations on Facebook.

"You've been calling me Old Man for quite some time," he said to Alise.

"Since you turned seventy," she said.

"No, longer than that."

It was a term of endearment from Alise and Pete took it as such.

She was in her second year at Nichols College, working at Market Basket in Oxford and Marshall's in the mall in Millbury and vaulting into adulthood as an ambitious, engaging and vivacious young woman. There was no trace of the Alise whose midsection was twisted in knots at one and two and three, who would wail incessantly in the living room of Pete and Mary Lou's home, her screeches so loud and so unrelenting that everyone worried about what could be causing such distress.

The bellyache that prompted these bouts eventually disappeared, replaced by a buoyant personality that carried her through her years as an Oxford High cheerleader and on into her twenties with the same strong urge to succeed as her older role models: sister Alexandra and cousins Cassandra, Jocelyn and Mitchell.

Maddie had whipped up a crock pot of pasta and meatballs, Pete's favorite meal. Alex had brought a salad.

Around the dining room table, as DJ lit the candles, Pete turned to Alise, and, looking into her eyes, which sparkled like jewels, said, "I have two thoughts to mark the occasion, granddaughter. First, whoever said that aging is only a state of mind didn't know what the hell they were talking about! Also (as he viewed with approval the smiles this remark had brought), the USS *Constitution*, Old Ironsides, anchored in Charlestown Harbor, the oldest warship in the U.S. Navy, turned two hundred twenty-two years old yesterday, on the same day I turned seventy-four…

"I'm just a spring chicken!"

II

Earlier that month, Pete had discovered that restaurateur Chris Liazos, just back from his every-other-year trip to Greece and now in his eighties, had been diagnosed with Stage 4 pancreatic cancer; the very same death sentence that loomed for Maddie's Claude. Cassandra and Kate had both worked for Chris Liazos at the Webster House. Pete's friendship with Chris had blossomed there. Pete and Mary Lou had attended Chris's seventy-fifth birthday party, hosted by Chris's wife Helena. Helena had passed away all too soon after that.

Now two of Pete's closest acquaintances—Chris Liazos and Joe Cutroni Jr.—were battling cancer. As was Claude Lucier.

The years, thirty-four of them since the Nash family had settled in Massachusetts, stretched behind Pete. Many of the people he had come to know as a newspaperman were gone including two of the best reporters who had worked under him at the *Blackstone Valley Tribune* in the late 80's. Both had died young.

Pete often paused to tick off the names of all who fell into this category.

He stopped what he was doing, frequently, too, to consider the tests to their endurance as a family that he, Mary Lou and the children had weathered.

He would from time to time take stock of his performance as a husband and father; as a son, brother, son-in-law, brother-in-law, uncle, cousin, nephew, colleague, friend. Asking himself, "how have I measured up? Has it been good enough?"

That his life and work had amounted to something suggested to him that the community viewed him with respect. Even now, writing two articles a week for a newspaper company out of Webster, he was in demand. A realtor had recently asked for Pete to tell the story of her twenty-five years in the industry. She remembered a glowing profile of her he had written years before when she was training for a road race. A man he had not known until now, Palmer Swanson of Douglas, had asked for Pete's services too, for a piece on a documentary film being made about an historic church in Slatersville, an old mill town in northern Rhode Island. A publicist for the expansion of a local library asked if Pete could cover the groundbreaking ceremony; when he showed up, camera and notebook in hand, she said "it's so good to have you back in Grafton!"

Pete had done all he could to stop second guessing himself about The Move. He had lost the job that brought him to Massachusetts and the one after that but he had persevered. He wasn't sure that Mary Lou, Maddie, DJ and Kate fully appreciated the resilience it had taken for him to recover from those blows. He knew too, however, that each of them had in his or her own way dealt with adversity as best they could.

Pete was now the Old Man, the most senior on the Nash side of the family. The father, grandfather and great grandfather whose greatest success was not of a professional but a personal nature.

This, when all was said and done, was the title he was most proud of.

Patriarch.

CHAPTER TWENTY-SIX
DJ AND LORETTA

Pete and Mary Lou were in a state of readiness for Christmas, their fifty-first as a couple. By Mary Lou's count eighteen people would cram their way into the Nash's small living room and dining room for Christmas breakfast, if everyone came. All four leaves had been put in the dining-room table.

Mary Lou's cinnamon-flavored "bubble bread" was certain to have mouths watering long before eleven o'clock.

They had spent the afternoon of Christmas Eve putting together Christmas bags: bark candy, fudge, tangerines, cashews, snack mix.

"I don't know how much longer I can do this," Mary Lou said. "Eighteen!"

They had forgone a tree a while ago. Space was too limited. Instead, Mary Lou placed a small ceramic Christmas tree that Maddie had bought for her on the two-drawer stand next to her recliner. Clustered around it were a miniature Santa and Mrs. Claus, a miniature cat, a miniature dog. A large poinsettia Pete had picked up at Home Depot, which he bought her every year, sat on the library table facing the outside wall. Its red petals were already falling but it still blazed with color.

The few Christmas cards they had received lay in a white bowl on the table. Wreaths hung in the windows. Wooden ornaments—rocking horses, camels, along with glass angels and other symbols of the season—were arrayed in front of and around a manager scene on a drop-leaf table Pete had gotten from neighbors at a yard sale.

Mary Lou was proudest of the tiny angels with the grandkids' names on them that sat in front of the manger. They were arranged in order of their ages. Unable to find angels with the last of the grandkids' names on them, Mary Lou had written them on herself, in black ink.

For the past week she had been feeding Christmas CDs into the stereo in the dining room: Alabama, John Denver, Lee Ann Womack, Reba McIntyre, Alan Jackson.

The driveway was clear of the coating of ice that had covered it for several days. Aided by temperatures that had soared into the high 50s, Pete had used his straight-edged steel shovel to pry the sheet loose.

"We don't need anyone falling," he said.

"I wonder if I'm going to get the checkered red-and-white tablecloth I asked for," Mary Lou said.

II

Christmas Day, 2019. Pete could feel the absence of DJ and Kate on this merriest of occasions. He had gotten used to burying his disappointment whenever they weren't around and so he made a pretense of appearing joyous upon opening the gifts he received—and watching others claim theirs.

He had after all asked for these as part of the Secret Santa arrangement the family was trying for the first time.

"Irish Spring soap!" he said. "Nana won't let me buy it, my skin gets so dry in the winter." This comment enticed laughter from the others, who had squeezed into the living room.

"A new Webster's Collegiate Dictionary!" He waved it over his head. "I'll pass this on to you, Alise!" He had been correcting her spelling when she sent a text message "I love you to" by responding "it's *too*, not *to* !"

He unwrapped the songbook he was hoping for. "An invitation to my inaugural concert with the guitar will be coming soon!" he said. "I've been practicing!"

He watched as Alise tried on a knee-length black winter coat with fancy buttons and a sash and smiled as she expressed delight. He chided Mitchell, who got a fifty-dollar Amazon gift card from Nana, for the elaborate steps he had taken to provide his mother with a wish list that identified him as a Wentworth student and that included links to various websites. "Who does that?" Pete asked. He liked poking fun at his grandchildren. He liked the rise his jabs would provoke in them.

Pete continued looking on as bags and boxes were taken up, opened, and tossed aside after their contents were removed.

"A lot of people," he thought. "A lot of commotion, a lot of laughter, a lot of noise, a lot of pleased faces.

"But no DJ and no Kate."

PETE did not see coming what happened next.

Two days after Christmas, he left the house early to pick DJ up from the MetroWest Medical Center in Natick. On the ride out, on the Mass Pike to Rt. 9 East and then Rt. 27 and Rt. 135 into Natick Center, he thought of DJ in the psych ward again, asking for meds that staff were reluctant to give him, refusing suggestions that he submit to a long-term rehabilitation program ("I'll lose my spot in Oxford," he said), requesting instead in a telephone call that Pete come and get him and bring him back to 266 Main St.

He had been at MetroWest only a few days, after going by ambulance to St. V's in Worcester and being transferred.

Pete thought of Kate, working again, this time at the Lowe's on Lincoln St. in Worcester, living sober with other women at Rhodes House on Northampton St., committed to her recovery, reconnecting with Evelyn whose support she had come so close to losing more than once.

Kate was taking an RTA bus back and forth, occasionally asking Pete for a lift when she had to go in early or stay late, talking about buying a car from an auto-detailer businessman Pete knew, talking about sharing an apartment with Evelyn.

Pete had an uneasy feeling about DJ's circumstances; and Kate's.

III

DJ was an easy mark for a woman like Loretta, just as he had been for Jennifer and before that Harmony. Troubled women with troubled pasts.

"Nothing good is going to come of DJ hooking up with Loretta," Pete thought.

Pete had almost immediately pegged Loretta as a conniver. He figured her to be five to ten years older than DJ. She was a plump woman who took no more care in her personal dress, which usually consisted of just a housecoat and flip flops, than she did with her hair, which invariably flew in all directions. Chain smoking had left her voice raspy as the blade of a file. Her brown eyes appeared to Pete to emote both warmth and heartlessness. "A bad combination" he thought.

Loretta Maynard was not well-liked by those with whom she shared quarters. She professed to be a Christian and lorded her faith over anyone who came within ten feet of her. Within days of meeting Pete, she commandeered him as someone who would tolerate her windy expostulations on whatever subject matter interested her at that particular moment. Claiming to be a former teacher and a longtime resident of Worcester, she welcomed the chance to exchange observations about the schools and "city life" with Pete.

At first, Pete did not see Loretta as a menacing figure. They even hit it off for a while. They could talk religion, politics, sports, books, the weather, business—on equal terms. He was disturbed only by her insistence on dominating the conversation, and her habit of diverging from one topic to another without so much as a shifting of gears. Pete would listen to her continuous stream-of-consciousness commentary on current events from his spot on the sofa opposite the one she occupied and wonder "what have I gotten myself into?"

Loretta's initial comportment toward DJ was to mother him, engendering in neither Pete nor DJ any inkling that her designs would soon bend in an entirely different direction; that they would in fact result in DJ's undoing.

Father and son deduced within the first several weeks of DJ's stay at 266 Main St. that Loretta's overtures were so oppressively directed toward them that they could not be seen as anything but an attempt to own their time and affection. They were aware that the rest of the house considered her to be a charlatan—someone to be avoided at all costs lest her pervasive ways rob them of their sanity. When Loretta gravitated to the parlor to watch TV there was an emptying out of that place. Several of the male residents—the musically inclined Jeff who wrote his own lyrics and played them on a six-string, and Dan, who otherwise maintained generally cordial relations with men and women alike (when he wasn't high on weed, or drunk)—so detested her that they went out of their way to make her feel unwanted.

But then there was what seemed to be Loretta's genuine interest in DJ's welfare, and that of Amory, when she was with her father. There was as well Loretta and DJ's mutual attraction to the Bible, religious literature, and prayer. It was not so surprising, then, that an affinity developed between them that overrode even DJ's reservations about her intentions.

Loretta's maternal instincts gave way to a need for DJ to be her boyfriend.

They began sleeping together.

"I'm being careful, though, dad," DJ said.

III

At first, when the banging on the wall in the room next to his became incessant, even in the wee hours, DJ would turn the music up. How he needed sleep! It had never come before 2:00 or 3:00 a.m. anyway, for years on end now, because of his insomnia. Loretta's pounding to get his attention, to lure him back to her after a disagreement, made it that much harder.

Loretta could pray with the best of them and this was her trump card and so they would kneel with a Bible open in front of them and Loretta would beseech the Lord to bless their relationship. By wooing DJ with food, with demonstrations of her fondness for Amory, with money, with cigarettes, with what passed for intelligent conversation, she overpowered his feeble will to resist. Loretta was at the door to DJ's room when Pete knocked, on a Thursday afternoon. He had come by to pick DJ up for appointments in Worcester. By this time Pete's patience with Loretta had worn thin. DJ had told him how she played mind games with him; took his keys, his wallet, his cell phone; buttered him up one minute and sabotaged him the next.

Loretta had planted herself squarely in the opening to the room. DJ, behind her, was swaying to rock music that had been cranked to an ear-splitting level, his eyes telling Pete that he had no clue what was going on.

"Really?" Pete thought. "She is going to deny me entrance?"

Pete wasn't sure how long she had been there, only that both of them had been drinking heavily and that the room was trashed.

"Whatever pretense she made of caring for him has long since been dispelled by actions she is taking that jeopardize his sobriety," Pete thought.

Pete pushed past her. He could feel her strength as her arms gave way.

"Let's go," Pete said. "Put on your coat."

DJ moved toward the small fridge. Loretta headed him off.

"At least she's not going to let him leave here with booze in his pocket," Pete thought.

Pete took DJ's keys.

"I need those," Loretta said. "I'm doing his laundry."

"No you don't," Pete said. "Hang onto it for him until he gets back."

Pete locked the door as they left, ignoring Loretta's muffled grumble in response.

CHAPTER TWENTY-SEVEN
'NOW AT LEAST SHE'S SAFE'

Kate was in wretched condition when Pete found her. Evelyn was with him. Kate would not get off the sofa in the apartment where she was holed up with two men she knew who had taken her in.

Pete was aghast at what he saw. Kate's long brown hair was unkempt and without its usual luster. Her face—the countenance Pete had gazed upon so often, with such appreciation for its beauty—was now tight and distraught. Her eyes did not have their typical glint but were dull—lifeless. Her shoulders slumped in despair (resignation?).

He thought, "she is not going to make it back this time. And less than a week from her forty-fifth birthday."

"Sit down, baby girl." Kate patted the cushions next to her.

"No," Pete said. "You are going to the ER."

Evelyn did not move but instead took her mother's hand. She brushed Kate's hair away from her face.

"She lied to us, sir," Jimmy said. "I didn't know she left a halfway house. I will do right by her, like I told you on the phone. I'm ex-military. My dad was too. U.S. Navy."

Pete allowed himself a glance at Jimmy. He could see that he was hurting, maybe from PTSD, maybe just from all the drinking he and Kate had been doing.

Jimmy's roommate Michael stood to one side in his ski cap. Pete recalled Michael telling him in a separate call that Jimmy was a deadbeat. He only kept him around to help with the rent.

Pete's exasperation with Kate was more than any of them including Evelyn could know. Pete was in no mood for Kate's shenanigans.

"Baby girl, you are so pretty. How did I get so lucky?"

Kate made no effort to leave her spot on the sofa.

"Come on, mom. I'll help you to the car," Evelyn said. "It's right outside."

"I'll go. Give me a shot."

"No," Pete said. "No more. Go willingly or I'm calling 911 and you can go by ambulance."

"Don't do that," Michael said. "I can't have the cops here."

Pete had no idea what he meant but Michael had said he was fighting for custody of his two kids. Or maybe because amid the mess that was the living room there were the drugs he might be dealing. Pete had pegged the two of them, Jimmy and Michael, as so like the kind of riffraff Kate always gravitated toward.

Pete kept thinking of what Jimmy had said to him on the phone. "I am a true person."

"What the hell is that supposed to mean?" Pete thought.

"One shot. Let me have it," Kate said.

Pete took his cell phone from the pocket of his pants and started to dial the number. Kate under the influence was impossible to deal with. Leave it to the EMTs.

Pete hated that Evelyn had to see her mother this way but at twenty now, a college girl with a job and her own transportation, which she had saved ten thousand dollars to buy, Evelyn was not going to let an incident like this set her back.

She was strong-willed, always had been. She was close to her cousins, especially Alise, Amory and Mitchell, but she guarded her space. Pete remembered how often, when the family was together, Evelyn would drift off to be by herself. Frequently she would disappear, go upstairs to use Pete's laptop, or to draw pictures. She kept even those who showered her with affection at an arm's length. Pete was glad that when it was just himself and Evelyn, she would open up to him. He thought of her accompanying him on walks, when Kate and Evelyn lived with Pete and Mary Lou. He remembered the time they were on Linwood St. in their sneakers and Evelyn said "midget door, dead ahead." She had taken note, on previous forays, of a less-than-normal-sized door next to the sidewalk that apparently served as an entrance to the basement of a house.

Evelyn loved her mama. She had been back and forth with both of her parents but she was more forgiving of behavior of Kate's that had hurt her. Pete understood that it was because they had fun together. Kate's winning personality and the hours they shared shopping or putting on make-up or listening to music or watching crime dramas on TV offset Kate's occasional blunders.

Once Evelyn told Pete "when she's drunk I call her Kate. When she's sober I call her mom."

At the hospital with Kate in a wheelchair, which Pete had requisitioned to get her inside, he told the woman that she was coming in for alcohol, depression "and she is talking suicidal."

"Why do you say that?"

"Because of what she's been saying, 'if I don't see you,' 'I love you,' 'tell my daughter I love her.'"

Pete knew from the many times he had been to the ER with DJ that alcohol poisoning alone was not enough of a reason for his son to get prompt attention.

Besides, it was true, Kate was scaring him with some of what she had been saying.

"Katherine, do you want to be detoxed?" the woman asked.

Kate did not at first seem to understand the question. Then, her head drooping, she nodded.

"Sign here."

The woman pushed a tablet at her.

Kate managed to write her initials. *K.N.*

"If I hadn't said she was threatening to end her life they wouldn't have taken her right in," Pete whispered to Evelyn, as a nurse led them through double doors and down a hallway "We'd be sitting here for hours with all these people with the flu.

"Besides, she's in bad shape. She's really sick.

"Now at least she's safe."

CHAPTER TWENTY-EIGHT
'I LOVE YOU, DAD'

At what appeared to Pete to be the very end, when it seemed to him that all was lost, he still held out hope for DJ. This, although all indicators pointed to DJ having finally hit rock bottom.

Pete could not bring himself to accept the outcome that was staring the two of them in the face.

He kept trying to intervene on DJ's behalf. He bought him a cell phone to replace the one he couldn't' find. He didn't want to think about how much money he had spent, the extent of the financial investment he had made, in repeated attempts to fend off the wolf at the door.

"You've done enough, dad," DJ said.

He was sitting on the edge of his half-made bed, his shaved head buried in his hands, choking back sobs.

"I don't know what to do. I'm a wreck."

DJ had promised to clean the room after he got out of the mental-health unit at the hospital in Webster. But it was still in the same state of neglect. The clear plastic bag full of empty beer cans and cigarette butts that DJ had said he would dump in the trash bin, outside, two days ago, was sitting where Pete had last seen it. A pile of dirty clothes still lay on the floor. The door of the tiny refrigerator was still open. The fridge itself was still unplugged—and empty.

"Kind of like his life, barren, devoid of any glimmer of optimism that tomorrow will be a brighter day," Pete thought.

Two weeks before, when Pete had shown up to find Loretta standing in his way, he had managed to get DJ to the psychiatrist's office on Belmont St.

There, the young doctor had said she couldn't help DJ, couldn't prescribe him anything, because he didn't have his paperwork with him.

"Of course he doesn't," Pete thought. "He was too drunk to remember it and it was my oversight not to grab it."

Now here Pete was back in the room, staleness hanging in the air even though DJ had the window cracked as he always did because the heat coming from the radiators was so oppressive.

Everything was the same except that Loretta wasn't there.

"She's in detox," DJ said.

"How pathetic," Pete thought.

"Did you eat the food mom sent you, the roast beef?'

"Yes, thanks.

"I don't know what to do."

"You need a program?"

"Yeah."

"You know how this works, DJ," Pete said. "You have to make the calls."

"I am."

Pete knew this wasn't true. DJ was lying to him.

"You have chicken cacciatore here, from your mother. Some cookies.

"Please eat."

"I don't know what to do."

"He's repeating himself."

Pete had been in this position before, when he had run out of answers. He remembered all those years ago when DJ was in his teens and dating Charlene, the picture of the two of them dressed like a king and queen for the middle school prom and then DJ standing in the driveway hours later, apologetic for getting smashed again.

"I am such a loser," he had said.

"No you're not," Pete had replied.

Pete knew there was only so much he could do.

"I have to be getting back. I will check on you tomorrow, okay? Call or text anytime."

"I love you, dad. Thanks for everything."

Pete walked into the cold night, closing the side door of the building behind him.

"It is January 16th," he thought.

"In six days DJ will turn forty-six.

"Or not."

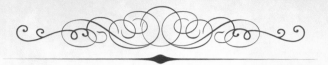

CHAPTER TWENTY-NINE
PEACE IN THE VALLEY

The song on the radio on January 20, 2020 spoke of "no more sadness, no more sorrow," but this did not lift Pete's mood at all. In fact it only made him more despondent.

The station was celebrating the legacy of Dr. Martin Luther King Jr. by playing a rich assortment of gospel and spiritual music. Pete was heading to All Saints Church on Irving St. to check out "Dreams of Harmony," one of a number of events around the city honoring Dr. King.

Driving along Park Ave., listening to 91.9 FM, he wished he could feel the "faith, hope and healing" that was being conveyed by the words of the mostly black artists who had been cued up for the audience's enjoyment that afternoon. He recalled that Lay Minister Sue Stone had addressed the same subject in her sermon in Oxford the day before, in standing in for Pastor Barry, who was on vacation.

Instead, Pete felt overwhelmed by the latest news involving DJ. This, coupled with Kate trying for sobriety—yet again—filled him with regret for what could have been but that remained beyond their grasp.

Pete hadn't heard from DJ since the previous Thursday evening. Desperate for any word, he and Maddie had stopped after church, on Sunday. The door to DJ's room was locked.

"The cops came by Friday night around 8:15," Mike, standing in the driveway, smoking, with the hood of his sweatshirt pulled over his head, told them.

Joe—"Jug"—stood alongside.

"Guns drawn. He called the police, said he was miserably depressed and that he had a knife."

Pete tried not to show his shock. He had never thought it would come to this, that DJ would resort to such tactics. "My son. My own flesh and blood, who I have tried to set an example for. How is it possible that my actions have not had the effect I intended?

"You don't know where they took him?"

"No," Mike said.

At the police station after a wait an officer emerged to report that DJ had been taken to UMass Medical's University Campus.

"I can't say any more than that, because of HIPPA," the officer said.

Pete thanked him, satisfied at least that DJ was getting the care he needed.

"Donald was discharged yesterday morning at 11:30," the woman on the telephone at the hospital said.

"Today is Monday," Pete thought, as he hung up. "That was twenty-four hours ago.

"Where is he?"

Pete could feel panic setting in. DJ's frame of mind, when Pete had last seen him, talked to him, had been worrisome. He had been adrift, refusing help.

"Now," Pete thought, "the temperature has dropped to 13 degrees."

Waiting for word was the hardest part; and this wasn't the first time.

II

In the sanctuary of All Saints, Pete listened as a black tenor, accompanied by a pianist, sang "Precious Lord" in a booming voice to a predominately white audience. Pete took several photos, intending to use them in some reflections on the significance of the day.

Leaving early in the program, he knew what he had to do.

Pete circled through downtown. The only people about on a quiet holiday were ones DJ was probably familiar with.

Driving slowly, Pete checked the usual spots. The Common. The Dunkin' Donuts at Harrington Corner. The area in and around Salem St. in the vicinity of the library. Main St. heading toward Main South. Lower Pleasant St. Temple St., even though the food pantry at St. John's, run by Billy Riley and Fr. Madden, wouldn't be open right now.

Pete remembered that he had seen a man sleeping in a portal of the old David Burwick Fine Furniture building at Chandler and Main, once. How, waiting at the traffic light, he had studied the man, curled in a lump in broad daylight, oblivious to life around him, and thought, "how I would hate to see DJ end up that way. He has come close, a few times."

Convinced that DJ was nowhere to be found, Pete turned right onto Myrtle St. from Salem St. and then left onto Southbridge St.

He wanted to look further but then he thought "what's the point?"

"If he needs me, he will get in touch.

"He always does."

Pete pointed the car south, toward Northbridge, and home.

EPILOGUE

April, 2020

Oh!' The exclamation from DJ, and his hand reaching for the dial of the car radio, gave Pete a start.

Pete was used to his son switching stations in the Nissan without asking to do so, and in fact repeating the process as he continued to cast about—like a fisherman dropping a baited line into different parts of a pond or stream in the hope of landing bass or trout—for a song he wanted to hear.

Pete allowed DJ this courtesy. He did not begrudge it to him, although his preference would have been for the number 91.9 not to change. This was DJ taking command, exerting authority, making decisions; proving himself capable of calling the shots. His illness—the disease of alcoholism—had stolen from him the can-do spirit he had once possessed to such an extent that it was now normally only apparent when he was landscaping. In the yard, DJ showed no hesitancy to dig and prune and fertilize and mow; he was in his element, comfortable explaining to his father what needed to be done—and when.

In most other situations, not so much.

Pete wished nothing more for DJ than for him to be able to drive again. He understood that in selecting the music they would be listening to, DJ was making up for his lack of a license to operate a motor vehicle. He was asserting what control he could. Which is also why, when talking on his cell phone to one of his girls or to his friend Johnny from the front passenger seat, he would say "I am heading your way."

I, replacing we. If it had been within his power to do so, Pete would have turned the wheel over to him. He was that certain that DJ would have handled the task responsibly.

"Syknyrd!"

The song "Simple Man," by Lynyrd Skynyrd, was No. 1 on DJ's all-time list. When he first played it for his father many years ago, when the words of a mama talking to her son—"oh, take your time, don't live too fast/troubles will come and they will pass/you'll find a woman and you'll find love/and don't forget, son, there is someone up above"— Pete could feel goose bumps form on his arms and his heart swell with empathy.

DJ had tried to live by the words of Lynyrd Skynyrd's Simple Man. He had tried to adhere to the admonition "forget your lust for the rich man's gold/all that you need is in your soul."

Pete knew how much the song meant to DJ. They had adopted it as an anthem of their love for one another. Whenever it came on, they were equally pleased.

It was not lost on Pete, however, that it was a mother, not a father, dispensing the advice. It very well could have been Mary Lou, notwithstanding the pain she had suffered. Yes, she was dubious of DJ's capacity to eventually turn away completely from alcohol and drugs, but Pete had no problem substituting Mary Lou for the mama in the tune, Mary Lou saying to DJ, as the unnamed mother does in the lyrics, "boy, don't you worry, you'll find yourself/follow your heart and nothing else/and you can do this, oh baby, if you try/all that I want for you, my son, is to be satisfied."

In more ways than even he would admit, DJ **was** the man in the song. Yes, he had fallen short of his own expectations. But aside from the slips, he had measured up to the challenge set forth by Ronnie Van Zant and the other members of a Florida rock band. He had kept close to his heart memories of his grandmothers, whose faith and generosity continued to inspire him. He had nurtured his daughters with equal parts tender mercies and firm reproaches as a stay-at-home dad when they were young—still, he said, the best job he ever had. He had expressed in rhyme his feelings toward loved ones and friends he had lost (now numbering more than twenty, with the recent death of a classmate and celebrated athlete, from an overdose). He had made Nature in all of its manifestations a centerpiece of his life. He had espoused the tenets laid out for him in The Big Book. He had always followed Christ's teachings in treating others with the same kindness he sought from them—and didn't always receive. Save for mention on occasion of his desire to become wealthy and live in Hawaii, he had not put much stock in the accrual of money. He had been "Pa Pa" to his grandson Tyler by building Lego structures with him and by searching under rocks in the yard for worms that Tyler could put in a jar. He had held Ned, and glowed with pride at the thought of a second grandson.

He had stood by his sisters. He didn't judge them when they faltered, as he had.

He never failed to kiss his mother goodnight.

DJ held Skynyrd's Simple Man up as the code of conduct he aspired to emulate.

"Donald Jeremiah, son of mine," Pete thought. "If he could only realize how close he has come to being that Simple Man. Of being that principled person who remembers to 'always be humble and kind'—as Tim McGraw advocates in a song that moves the two of us, whenever we hear it.

"I am so proud of him."

II

At the sober house at the corner of North and Sigourney streets in Worcester, where she was again fighting her way back from a low, Katherine Rose seized the offer to talk about her brother, when it was extended, in a group chat.

Kate was sitting amid a dozen or so other women, all of them quarantined because of the coronavirus that had raged its way across the globe in early 2020. With her usual penchant for frankness, she had posted a photo of herself on Facebook, masked, with the message "ridiculous. We are not allowed to go anywhere but they want us to wear face coverings as protection? From what? Seriously?"

DJ would have been aghast at this impertinence from his sister. They were very different in that regard. DJ seldom bucked in protest, like a wild horse would—against authority. In all of his run-ins with the law, he had submitted to the iron will imposed on him by the arresting officer. He had respect for their role in society—the job they had to do. This is why, Pete knew, he hadn't been guilty of assaulting Benny Emerson, when that charge was thrown at him all those years ago in Uxbridge District Court. Violence of any sort ran counter to his instincts. Unlike Kate, too, he seldom forced his thoughts on others during animated debate; he was content to sit and listen. He was less demonstrative than his "little sis." He was certainly a whole lot less confident too.

Now Kate as her turn came up was relating to her housemates the great love she had for DJ.

"My big bro has always looked out for me," she said. "When we were just little kids, mom and dad took us to Front Street Days in Vestal. It's like a bazaar, it's held in the summer. There are vendors on both sides of the road. Makeshift tents everywhere. Very festive. We hadn't gotten far on the sidewalk, the five of us walking along together, holding hands. It was hard to move, there were so many people. At that age I was known for disappearing on a moment's notice. Which is exactly what happened. Before anyone knew it, I was way ahead, mixed in with total strangers who stood three times my height. I was totally unconcerned about the anxiety I had caused. That's when I heard DJ's cry. I can still hear it today, DJ beside himself with worry, shouting through his sobs 'my parents have lost my sister!'

"That was so like him. He and I, we have been through a lot. We are both alcoholics of course. I can't tell you how many times he has given me a pep talk, told me I can beat this. If I'm in trouble, he hurts. I know he does. Dad tells me DJ is always asking about me, wondering how I'm doing.

"I know I disappoint him when I crash, but he understands. His struggle has been my struggle. Here in Worcester, in grade school, in middle school, he was the one who was picked on but he made sure no one messed with me.

"He hasn't always approved of my lifestyle but he never holds that against me. He just wants me to be okay."

Kate paused to collect herself. She could see that she had the room in tears.

"There is nothing that my big bro wouldn't do for me.

"I am not sure which of us is the worst alcoholic. Our urge to drink doesn't come from the same place, exactly. It's a buffer for both of us but for him it stems from a deep depression where in my case it's more of a desire to get the most out of social settings. DJ doesn't drink to be a party animal. He drinks to drown out his sorrows. Me, I have many of the same reasons as him to want to pick up, because of the trauma we suffered moving to Massachusetts. I don't know if either of us will ever put it down for good.

"I do know that DJ will never desert me.

"I love my big bro, always have, always will."

III

At least twice within a span of a half dozen or so years, right up to the present, Madeline Anne had not been able to resist the compulsion to remind her father of the indignities she had suffered as a consequence of his actions.

The first time, Maddie was cleaning up after Easter dinner at her home. She was at the kitchen sink, her back to members of the family, who were sitting and conversing at the dining room table—several feet away.

Pete was engaged with Claude's parents in a discussion of turmoil in the Worcester Public Schools; specifically, a recent spate of incidents involving students at the new North High. In one of these, a boy had assaulted an assistant principal immediately after last bell. The news had sent shock waves through the community.

"The city spent millions putting up that building but the problems that were there before, for staff and teachers, still exist," Pete said. "Nothing's changed."

Hearing her father's remark, Maddie stopped what she was doing and, casting a glance over her shoulder and with her eyes bristling in anger, said, "thanks, dad! I was scared to death!"

Pete did not respond. But in that instant he felt both chagrin for having been reprimanded so long after the fact—and appreciation for his daughter stating in such emphatic terms how she felt.

"She has every right," he told himself. "If I were able to put myself in her shoes, back in September and October of 1985, I would have been just as terrified of my surroundings. I remember what it was like, in going for my own sophomore year from Jennie F. Snapp to Union-Endicott High School; from a school I knew well, that I felt comfortable and content in, where I played on the freshman basketball team, where I experienced my first dates, to a school that seemed so big—so imposing."

The second example that Maddie had not completely let go of the past came in the spring of 2020 when, chatting with Pete and Mary Lou on a Monday visit to her parents' home, she and her mother reminisced about the house on Hoffman Ave. in Vestal.

"You loved that house," Maddie said. "I did too."

"That was my house," Mary Lou said.

The family had lived there only briefly. Maddie was old enough when Pete's father built it to remember every detail. She knew that Mary Lou had insisted on a laundry room on the first floor, right off the kitchen, despite "dad Nash's" protestations that she would be giving up needed space. She remembered too the day that the men of the family got together in barn-raising fashion to replace the dirt driveway with a concrete surface. Horace Nash had set the forms for the project, and ordered the cement from a company he was used to working with. Horace, Pete, Pa Jenkins, Pete's brother-in-law's Lucas and Joe and Pete's brothers Roy and Kent spent the whole morning and afternoon guiding the ooze as it poured from the chute of the big truck into the 10 x 80-foot opening—from the street all the way up to the detached garage.

Maddie remembered too Horace Nash constructing the front porch. She remembered her grandfather, in his apron and with a carpenter's pencil in his ear, hammering the rails and the spindles into place.

She remembered when her parents finished the basement. She remembered taking piano lessons in the den. She remembered family meals in a dining room created exclusively for that purpose. She remembered her parents playing Pinochle with Bob and Cheryl Klingensmith at the table in the kitchen. She remembered the Thomas boy, to the left, and the O'Brien boy, to the right.

She remembered it all.

She had thought long and hard about what her father had walked away from, what must have motivated him to undertake his Don Quixote-like quest for a supposed better life.

This was all behind her now. Like her mother, her brother and her sister, Maddie had tried to make sense of The Move. This had proven fruitless. Only her father, Pete Nash, could explain it and even then that would not be to anyone's satisfaction.

Maddie no longer dwelled on how things might have turned out for her if the family had stayed in Vestal. Thirty-five years after her aborted bid to flee, with a husband who was in failing health, with three grown children who sustained her belief in the sanctity of motherhood, with parents she loved, with a brother and sister she cared deeply for, with a home that was her refuge, with nieces and nephews she adored, with a church and a congregation from which she drew sustenance, she had managed to squeeze something tangible out of prospects that had looked so unpromising to begin with.

Her grandfathers, her grandmothers, had passed on years ago. She hadn't been back to Broome County, to Vestal, in some time.

She would never forget where she came from. Or what her father took from her.

She had learned to live with it.

IV

At seventy-two years of age, Mary Lou reveled in a love for her husband that compensated for the disappointments he had subjected her to.

No two people, on the surface, would have seemed to be so seriously mismatched. Even to those who knew them well, they must have appeared as the oddest of couples. Their personalities were as different as night and day. From the moment Pete roused her in the morning until she put her book away and turned off the light in the living room around midnight, her mind was fixated on problem solving. Whether putting together slices of banana and orange in just the right manner for a small fruit cup, working her way through the word puzzle in the newspaper, repairing a rip in jeans for Amory with needle and thread, striving to bake an apple pie that was better than her last effort, figuring out how to record more than two shows at the same time on television or attempting to manufacture a face mask from coffee filters as a counter to the outbreak of Covid-19, her concentration was almost entirely devoted to the rudimentary tasks that would make life flow more smoothly.

"You are your father's daughter," Pete would tell her.

Pete's attention, in sharp contrast, gravitated toward endeavors that would satisfy his desire to create prose worthy of notice. She may not have understood the inordinate number of hours he dedicated to this pastime. But she allowed him the opportunity to exercise his craft in the AM, as he allowed her the afternoons she spent catching up on cooking shows—or an episode of "Grey's Anatomy" or "Chicago Fire."

Increasingly, Pete thought, their lives had diverged. Their preferences—in books, in music, to some extent in TV programming, in what they perceived as humorous, in who they wanted to associate with in terms of friends—bent more and more away from each other.

Had Pete been asked "what makes your marriage work," he would have been tempted to answer "opposites attract."

But there was also a compatibility that could not be denied.

Pete knew exactly what he had in Mary Lou (Jenkins) Nash.

Which was, a woman who had surrendered much of herself to keeping him fed, nursed, amused, entertained, uplifted—and forgiven.

Mary Lou often said to him "you should have married someone more fun."

His response was always, "no, I made the right choice."

V

Pete did not focus on the regrets, although he, like Mary Lou, Maddie, DJ and Kate, had his share. His were not the same as theirs. He knew he had gained more from life in Massachusetts than them. This precluded any desire he might have had to confront Mary Lou with sentiments other than the ones of a positive type that he typically put forth to her—and to his children.

Of paramount importance too, overriding all other considerations, was the action he had taken that initiated the whole business: that felled the first domino, triggering, as it toppled, the collapse of the rest.

It would have been hard for Pete Nash to justify the impulses that set the wheels of the carriage, rolling east, in motion. What had transpired—the sequence of events that had amounted to a net loss for the family—could not be disputed. Or changed. The first of these, Maddie's brazen refusal to go along with his vision, had been followed in rapid succession by the car accident, the fire, DJ and Kate's descent into a dependence on drugs and alcohol, Pete's loss of the job in Brookline, DJ's strained relationship with Kylie and his ongoing battle to win custodial rights for visits with his daughters from her, Maddie's brief questioning of her self-worth, the disintegration of her marriage, the diagnosis of advanced pancreatic cancer for Claude and an estrangement between Mary Lou and Kate—punctuated by Mary Lou's refusal to speak to her daughter—that hung in the air like an exclamation point at the end of a sentence.

Pete Nash had been held to account for his role in the Nash family saga. He thought of it more often than his wife and children realized—even after it had ceased to be an issue, for the most part.

Few days went by when he didn't think about how he had benefitted while they had not.

He could only hope that his actions as a husband and father had finally balanced the scales.

As a continuing penance, he could see his saintly maternal grandmother, Blanche, his ever-so-gracious mom, Beatrice, and yes his ever-dutiful father, Horace Nash—who had built Mary Lou's forever house—looking on and saying to him "why were you thinking only of yourself, For Pete's Sake?"

ABOUT THE AUTHOR

Rod Lee was born in Endicott, New York, one of four children, all boys. He and his brothers were the sons of a framing carpenter and a homemaker/bookkeeper.

In 2004, he published a memoir of his youth, *Shoe Town,* that was hailed by readers from coast to coast as an accurate and nostalgic depiction of a village built on the generosity of George F. Johnson and the company he founded: Endicott-Johnson.

Many of these admirers of *Shoe Town* worked for EJ, or were sons, daughters or grandchildren of people who were employed in the Johnson family's factories.

Shoe Town also celebrated the football teams of Union-Endicott High School and the firebrand of a coach, Fran Angeline, for whom victory—and manhood—were an all-consuming passion.

For Pete's Sake—the saga of Pete Nash and his wife Mary Lou and their children Madeleine, Donald Jeremiah ("DJ") and Katherine, in the traumatic move they made from small-town New York to bustling Worcester, Massachusetts—is the author's sixth book.

He resides in Linwood, Massachusetts with his wife, Marie.
rodlee.1963@gmail.com

Printed in the United States
By Bookmasters